26/8/91

IN HER GARDEN

IN HER GARDEN

GARDEN

JON GODDEN

ALFRED A. KNOPF

NEW YORK 1981

THIS IS A BORZOI BOOK
PUBLISHED BY ALFRED A. KNOPF, INC.

Copyright © 1981 by Jon Godden
All rights reserved under International and
Pan-American Copyright Conventions.
Published in the United States by Alfred A. Knopf, Inc.,
New York, and simultaneously in Canada by
Random House of Canada Limited, Toronto.
Distributed by Random House, Inc., New York.

Library of Congress Cataloging in Publication Data

Godden, Jon, [date]   In her garden.
I. Title.
PR 6013.01815   823'.914   80-19849
ISBN 0-394-51361-4   AACR1

Manufactured in the United States of America
First Edition

IN HER GARDEN

CHAPTER

1

The swallows were back. Grace looked up from the box of seedlings she was planting and saw them flashing across the sky. The birds were late—wise birds, for it had been bitterly cold and wet for months; today was the first true spring day and warm for early May. Yes, the swallows were back, with their promise of summer; they wheeled and swooped round the tiled roofs of the house, celebrating their arrival and the end of a long and perilous journey before getting down to the business of nest building. She smiled as she watched them, and thought of the way they had come, thousands of miles, across deserts and seas, over the Alps.

The birds did not have the sky to themselves. Far above them, a plane moved steadily across the blue from east to west, shining as the sun caught it; the drone it made reverberated on the air. At once she imagined herself up there, looking down on the green countryside and the village spread out beneath her like a map. All the guide-books' descriptions applied: the old houses huddled round the Green among the trees in their gardens, the church tower, squat and dwarfed from that height, rising among them, then the houses of the council estate and the new bungalows spreading like a rash across the fields. There was the big house, now a preparatory school, in its park, and the caravan site on the other side of the village. She looked down on the pink walls of her own house, Setons, standing aloof a mile away, and at the plan of her garden, every inch of which she knew so well. She saw her white-haired self, old Mrs. Maitland, in her faded blue gardening clothes, kneeling by the border in the side garden. Feeling slightly giddy, as if from a real descent, she returned to earth.

What am I doing, wasting time dreaming, when I'm so behindhand in the garden? she asked herself. After I have finished this box, I must get down to some weeding.

The hours passed unnoticed, as time always did when she was gardening.

"Mother! Where are you?"

Grace raised her head. Her hand in its gardening glove paused in its work. Perhaps if I keep very still, she thought, Dilys won't see me kneeling here. Perhaps she will go away.

The voice came again, louder, nearer, and she sighed. She had planned to spend the whole day in

4

the garden, which so badly needed attention. What can Dilys want? she thought. It's not long since she was here and we had that scene, and then she remembered that, feeling contrite because she had been so disagreeable, she had asked her stepdaughter to come again in a week's time. "If you insist, we can discuss it then when our tempers have cooled," she had said, "but it's no use. I won't budge."

Still holding her trowel, she stood up, with some difficulty because kneeling made her stiff. It was true, as Dilys was so fond of reminding her, that she was not as young as she had been. Who is, after all?

Dilys was walking in her determined way down the path. Even at that distance Grace could see that she looked cross, and her heart sank. The sun shone on Dilys's bare head with its thick dark short hair, which had no grey in it although she was well past forty. She was a big handsome woman—handsome was the right word for her. What a funny solid little girl she had been; a silent child but emotional, given to easy tears. Grace, when she married Hubert Maitland, had been afraid that a stepmother would be resented. Far from it. From the first, Dilys, who could not remember her own mother, had attached herself to Grace, following her about everywhere, as persistent as a big burr and, like a burr, irritating, impossible to shake off. "Thank God the child has taken to you," Hubert had said. How like her father Dilys had become. It was a pity that she had the same rather heavy legs. If I were she, Grace thought, I would wear trousers, at any rate in the country. Still, she looks very elegant, as she always does. I like that new short coat.

"So there you are, Mother. I might have known that you would be somewhere in the garden. Have you any idea of the time? It's after one and you said half-past twelve."

"Did I? Does it matter on such a lovely day? Let's go back to the house and have a drink."

Grace laid her trowel down, took off her gloves, and kissed her stepdaughter, something she seldom did. She was feeling guilty because, as far as she knew, there was nothing for lunch except eggs. It will have to be an omelet, she thought, it usually is an omelet, and then Dilys will know that I have forgotten again.

She said, "Do you mind if we go round by the kitchen garden? It won't take a minute. I've some lettuces ready. You would like a salad, wouldn't you?"

"Yes, if there is something else as well. I'm famished."

As they went together into the main garden and crossed the lawn in front of the house, Grace said, "It's good of you, Dilys, to drive all this way to see me when you are so busy."

"Of course it isn't *good* of me. I like seeing you, and Desmond and I worry about you, all alone in this big house. I wish you were nearer, but it isn't really far, only fifty miles."

"Was the traffic very bad?"

In Her Garden

"Terrible. It's a nightmare getting out of London these days. I thought I was going to be late—not that it would have mattered to you, would it?"

"No, dear," Grace said in the vague way that so annoyed her stepdaughter. She opened the door in the wall that bounded the kitchen garden and led the way up the path between the espaliered pears towards the greenhouses and the row of frames. "Here we are," she said. "Choose your own lettuce. They are a fine lot, aren't they? And only me to eat them. Why not take some back to Desmond? He would appreciate something really fresh."

"I'll take two, that's enough. Now, come on, Mother. I'm dying for that drink. What are you staring at?"

"Nothing. I was only thinking how much I like this walled garden—that old red brick, such a colour."

"It's full of weeds, overgrown."

"Don't, Dilys. It distresses me very much to see it in such a state. To think that once, when you were a little girl, we had two men and a boy on the place."

"I know, you've told me. How do you think you're going to manage now that old Martin has given up?"

"I don't know, but I will."

"If you stay here, you'll have to get someone else."

"I've tried. It's not so easy. There seem to be very few gardeners about."

"Did you arrange for that firm, Lawns Limited, or whatever they are called, to mow the lawns at least?"

"Yes, and to cut the hedges. I couldn't begin to manage those, there are so many."

"You'll still need more help if you're not going to kill yourself. Surely you could get a man to do the rough work, digging and so on. That would be something."

"It would indeed. A man's hands, that's what this garden needs. I'll ask Mrs. Barrett again."

"She still comes regularly?"

"Four mornings a week on her moped, bless her. Half-past nine to half-past twelve. It means that I do practically no housework, which I hate."

"All the same, the house is too big for you. It's ridiculous these days."

Grace did not answer. The last thing she wanted was another argument and she didn't mean to have one, not before luncheon anyway.

"We'll go in the back way," she said, and they crossed the yard, backed by a range of outhouses that had once been stables and now were garages, in one of which her Mini sat in lonely state. The door from the yard led through a lobby where the backstairs emerged, into a scullery and kitchen. Grace thought once again how odd it was that when she was alone the house seemed to be exactly the right size and to fit her perfectly, especially now that she had closed those unnecessary rooms, but when Dilys was there it expanded and confused her by seeming bigger than it really was. Today the stone-flagged scullery looked vast and so did the kitchen. She knew what Dilys was going to say, and she said quickly, "The drinks are in the morning-room. We'll eat there; I always do now that I've closed the dining-room, which was far too big for me."

"I would like a wash first."

"So would I, and I had better change these trousers, they are a bit grubby. Come up to my room."

The hall was not really large, but it had a spacious air, as had all the rooms in the house. She had left the front door open that morning because it was such a fine day and it seemed a pity to shut out the view over the drive to the distant hills; sunlight lay across Hubert's treasured rugs. The curve of the staircase never failed to please her, although she must have climbed it thousands of times. "I have lived in this house the greater part of my life, ever since I married," she said, before she could stop herself.

Dilys said promptly, "I know, but nothing lasts forever, Mother. You must make up your mind."

"It's made up."

She heard Dilys sigh, an exasperated sound, and as Grace opened her bedroom door she asked, "How are the children?"

Usually any mention of her children was enough to divert Dilys, but today she only answered briefly, "They're all right, I hope."

"Anne still in Paris?"

"Yes, until the end of the summer."

"Learning some French, I trust, and David?"

"He's working very hard, or so he says. A Levels."

In Her Garden

"Poor thing. Life is hard for the young now—all these A's and O's. Thank goodness I escaped all that."

"Mother, please listen."

"Yes, dear. But let's wait until after lunch. I hope there's a clean towel in the bathroom."

The bathroom led out of her bedroom as did Hubert's dressing-room. As she changed her trousers, Grace looked round her, at the three windows, the huge double bed, the old-fashioned dressing-table, and the chaise-longue that had belonged to Hubert's mother. It's a lot of space for one woman, she thought, too much, selfish and wrong in these congested times. And then she thought, I hate small rooms. After all this I should stifle in a flat. I won't even think of it.

Luncheon was over. Grace had made coffee and carried the tray out onto the terrace, where they could sit and look over the expanse of lawn to distant yew hedges and the two stone urns at the top of the steps leading down to the rose garden. The old argument was still going on.

"I wouldn't be happier in a flat, Dilys. I should hate to live without a garden."

"You could have window-boxes, perhaps a little roof garden."

Grace snorted, a small contemptuous sound that made Dilys flush with annoyance.

"How selfish you are, Mother. You don't care a bit that Desmond and I are so worried about you."

"You needn't worry. I'm still capable of looking after myself and will be for years yet. When I'm eighty, it may be different. Perhaps I'll listen to you then."

"You're over seventy."

"Seventy-five, as you well know. I don't consider that old. I don't feel old and I'm as strong as a horse."

"You're much too thin. I don't believe you eat enough."

"I've just eaten quite a substantial lunch."

"What would you have had if I hadn't been here? An apple and a glass of milk?"

"Very likely. Quite enough too."

Dilys sighed. "You must be lonely by yourself in this big house. I hate to think of you alone here at night, especially since Goliath died—a Great Dane is some protection. If you insist on staying here you should get another dog."

"It wouldn't be fair at my age to take on another big dog, and what would be the use of a small one? I'm probably safer here than I would be in a London flat, and I've too much to do to be lonely. I've lived here alone ever since your father died and that's ten years. I still miss him, but, no, I'm never lonely."

"If only you would have a companion, someone to be around. Suppose you were suddenly taken ill?"

"I would ring up Hugh. He would be here in a few

minutes and you must admit I couldn't have a better doctor. As for a companion, surely the breed is almost extinct? I should hate to live with another woman."

"She would do your shopping for you. You know how much you dislike shopping, and she could drive the Mini. A car is essential here, over a mile from the village and only one bus a day. How much longer will you be able to drive?"

It was Grace's turn to be annoyed. "What nonsense! My driving is as good as ever; how can you say such a thing? I know—you're thinking of that silly little accident last week. I just grazed the gatepost, my own gatepost too. I wish I hadn't told you."

"No need to raise your voice like that, Mother. I'm going to say what I think."

"Very well, say it, once and for all, and then let's hear no more about it."

Grace leaned back in her chair, gazed at her stepdaughter, and prepared to listen. Her attention soon strayed. Dilys is good, she thought. She would do anything for me, she has been almost like a real daughter to me. I love her in a way, I suppose, but I can't like her. She irritates me, rubs me the wrong way . . . what a pity . . . Dilys was speaking earnestly. It was ungrateful not to listen.

"Setons will soon be too much for you, it's too much now. Desmond and I think you ought to make the break at once, before you are too old to adjust easily. Why wait? Everyone is retrenching these days."

"I can still afford this place, if that's what you

mean. My income doesn't go as far as it used to, no one's does, but there's always the capital."

"That would be foolish."

"Why? Hubert left his money equally between the two of us, and apart from Desmond, who is doing very well, you have your mother's money. I needn't worry about you or the children and I have no one else."

"It's not only the expense, it's the work. Do be sensible, Mother."

"If it means leaving this place, I won't be sensible, as you call it. What sense would there be in making myself miserable before I must?"

Grace stood up and began to walk up and down the terrace. She was a tall woman and had always been slim. Now, as Dilys had said, she was too thin and there was a deceptively frail air about her; her luminous grey eyes, set wide apart in their deep sockets, were too big for her face; sometimes she looked as if a puff of wind could be enough to blow her away like a leaf. Pausing by the table again, she looked down at her stepdaughter and said, "Your father loved this house and garden. He wouldn't want me to desert them."

"He wouldn't want you to make yourself ill trying to do more than you can. You would have time for your painting. You could travel."

"And where would I find flowers to paint in a flat? Bought flowers wouldn't be the same. I paint them as they are, growing in the garden."

"There are gardens in other countries."

In Her Garden

"Travelling is no fun these days. Too many people, no peace or comfort. I travelled a great deal once. Your father's business took him all over the world and I usually went with him. I've had the best of it and now all I want to do is to stay where I am."

There was a pause, then Dilys said, "Very well, I'll say no more. What's the use? You are an obstinate old woman and you must go your own way, I suppose. I've done what I can." The way she set the coffee cups down on the tray showed how annoyed she was.

"Don't be cross," Grace pleaded. "Just let me be. No one can arrange someone else's life for them, even if that someone is old."

"Desmond will be very put out," Dilys said, as she picked the tray up and carried it into the house.

"I doubt it," Grace said, following her. "He'll say, 'You've done your best, dear,' and then he'll forget all about it. I know Desmond."

Dilys, having washed up, said that she might as well go home where she could be of some use. She refused Grace's suggestion of a rest in the garden followed by tea, and fetched her coat.

Grace went with her across the hall and out onto the drive. "A new car?" she asked. "What was wrong with your Rover?"

"It was two years old and heavy on petrol. We turned it in for this MG. I've only had it a few days."

"It looks very sumptuous. I'm not sure about the colour though."

"Nor am I. I wanted a dark green but that would have meant waiting for months."

"Never mind, you'll soon get used to it. You look very grand in it, Dilys, sitting there behind the wheel. Most expensive."

"Goodbye, Mother. I'll ring you up in a few days. Meanwhile, do your best to find someone for the garden. You simply must."

"I'll put an advertisement in the shop tomorrow. Don't worry, someone is sure to turn up sooner or later."

"And you'll think over all I said, won't you?"

"Yes, dear," Grace said. "Thanks for coming. Give my love to Desmond."

As the car vanished down the drive and she turned back to the house, she said to herself, I shan't give it another thought.

Dilys was even more annoyed than Grace had realized. I'm beginning to hate Setons, she thought, and as for that garden—Grace loves it more than she loves anyone; I don't believe she can love anyone. Sometimes I think she only married Father because of the garden.

At the bend of the drive, out of sight of the house, she stopped the car and sat for a few moments with her hands on the steering-wheel, trying to calm herself and to make up her mind what she would tell Desmond. "Well?" he would say. "I was right,

In Her Garden

wasn't I? It was a waste of time. Why can't you leave
Grace alone?" As she drove on slowly, she remembered Desmond saying, "Dilys, are you jealous—jealous of a garden?" When she had protested, perhaps
too loudly, although she had tried to laugh at such an
idea, all he had said was, "I think you are, my dear."

Grace paused for a moment in the hall, which seemed
to her to hold the echo of Dilys's voice, and waited
for the customary silence to descend. It was half-past
three, plenty of time left in which to finish her weeding, but she was tired, limp from too much arguing.
Dilys always leaves me feeling much older, she
thought, and wandered through the drawing-room
with its ornamental ceiling and cabinets holding Hubert's collection of china, a beautiful room she seldom
used, except in the evenings when she sometimes
played the piano to amuse herself. Touching the
grand piano as she passed it, she went through the
long windows out onto the terrace. When Hugh had
given her a check-up last month, "just to be on the
safe side," he had advised her to rest every afternoon.
"Half an hour flat will do," he had said. This advice
she usually ignored. The sun had almost left the terrace, but it was a warm afternoon and she lay down
on her long, cushioned chair in the shadow of the
house. Above her the wistaria was in pale bloom; a
few petals drifted down.

"I'm never lonely," she had said to Dilys, and that
was true most of the time. It was many years since

she had taken any part in the doings of the village although she still went to the annual flower show. Most of Hubert's and her friends in the neighbourhood had died or moved elsewhere and she seldom, if ever, saw those who were left. She was content that this should be so, but perhaps only true hermits or mystics can live always alone. The rest, even those who liked solitude as much as she did, needed some human contact now and then. Only that morning, as she had knelt by the border, she had wished for a moment that there was someone she could turn to and say, "Look! The swallows are back."

When Dilys had arrived that moment was gone and she had felt only annoyance at the interruption. She had told Dilys that she still missed Hubert. Was that altogether true? He had been a tie and very tiresome and demanding in his old age. Could it be that what she missed was a man's presence about the place? At times, when she felt the need of someone to talk to, she would ring up Hugh but she did not do this often as he was a busy man. No one can talk to Mrs. Barrett, she thought, only listen to that flow of gossip, and closed her eyes.

When Grace woke, she sat up shivering. The sun still shone on the garden, but she was chilled through. She stood up, wondering what had roused her, some sound, she thought. She heard it again, faint but unmistakable. A car was coming up the drive.

She hurried through the house and out to the front steps. It was not a car. A shabby, rattling white van was turning in the drive. The back doors, not quite closed, were tied together with a length of rope, and she glimpsed some kind of lawn-mower and a collection of gardening tools. A fair-haired young man got out and, after hesitating a moment, came slowly towards her. "Someone is sure to turn up," she had said to Dilys.

When Grace first saw Ben Halden she thought he was far younger than she later discovered him to be. There was a youthful awkwardness about him and when he reached the steps and looked up at her, his blue eyes were clear and candid, as trusting as a child's. Innocent was the word that came into her mind, an odd word for such a large, solid young man.

"Mrs. Maitland?"

It was said diffidently, and to encourage him she smiled. "Yes, I'm Mrs. Maitland."

"Dr. Grainger sent me. He said as how you could do with some help in the garden. I work for him one day a week."

"I could indeed, as much time as you can give me, but I expect you're very booked up."

He smiled back at her then, a slow smile that lightened his rather heavy face. "Not yet. Only the doctor, Wednesdays. I've only just started. Bought the van a week ago." He turned his head and gave it a proud glance which she found touching.

"So you're setting up as a free-lance gardener?"

In Her Garden

"Jobbing gardener, they call it."

"What do you charge?"

"Pound fifty an hour. Seemed about right."

Would he be able to make a living? It was no business of hers, but she said, "Have you a family? Are you married?"

He looked away from her and she thought that his face changed, became closed and expressionless, as he answered, "Yes, I'm married." After a pause he added in a very different voice, "I've got a son. Five years old," and smiled his warm attractive smile again.

"Have you thought of working for Lawns Limited? They are always on the look out for men and they pay well. It would mean a regular wage."

"That's what the wife said. I'd rather be on my own. I'll do all right once I get started."

Perhaps he would. Diffident, awkward, he might be, but there was an air of quiet strength about him, and surely no one willing to work in a garden need ever be unemployed, not in her part of the country anyway. She would have been willing to pay him double what he was asking. She said, "Well, you can start here any time. I'll show you round the garden now so that you can see what needs to be done."

As they went together through the archway that led from the drive into the side garden, Grace was very conscious of him at her side. Although he was not much taller than she, he give the impression of being a big man, a large, calm, solid creature who gave out a comfortable animal warmth that she could almost feel. The fair, thin skin of his face and bare arms was already reddened by the day's sun, giving him a glowing ruddy look. In another of her surreptitious side glances she saw that his hair just touched the collar of his shirt and that his eyebrows and lashes were lighter than his hair; she had always disliked pale eyelashes, but they suited him.

Grace was not a curious woman and took most people for granted, yet she could not help wondering about this man. She saw now that he must be at least in his late twenties and here he was eager to employ himself full time in work usually done by old-age pensioners or boys waiting for something better to turn up. She tried gently to find out all she could about him.

He was willing, even eager, to talk about the garden, of which he seemed to approve. They were standing above the flight of steps that went down to her circular rose garden when he said, "Nice place you've got here. I like it." He turned to look at the lawn that stretched behind them to the house and then back to where a gap in the encircling yew hedges showed a vista of park-like meadows. He was reluctant, though, to tell her anything about himself, and he answered her questions almost curtly. She did not know why she persevered, but by the time they reached the kitchen garden she had at least learned his name and that his son was called Peter. He had moved his family a month ago to the village where his wife had relations and they were living in a caravan on the Site until they could get a council house.

His face lit up when he saw the big greenhouses,

which she had managed to keep in good order although there was not much in them except her pelargoniums and the boxes of seedlings she had spent hours yesterday pricking out.

"Have you always been a gardener?" she asked, watching his face.

"Always wanted to be."

It was then, in a rush of confidence, induced perhaps as much by the warm atmosphere of the greenhouse as by her sympathy, that he told her about his father who had been head gardener at a big house. As a child, and later as a boy, Ben had helped him in the greenhouses after school, working beside him, following him about, learning all the time and never doubting that he too would be a head gardener some day. His father, though, had had other plans for him. "Trouble was I hadn't the brains," Ben said. "No good at exams. Big disappointment I was," and he added, as if he were talking to himself, "Always have been."

After a moment she asked, "What did you do then?"

"Left home to begin with."

"And when you married?"

"Not enough money in gardening then. Tried my hand at this and that, couldn't get suited. Ended up working in a factory, food processing they did. Good money but after a time I couldn't stand it."

He was growing restless and she knew it would be foolish to ask any more questions, although she longed to know where he had got the money for the van. She said, "I think you're wise in these hard times to branch out as you are doing."

"Do you? No one else seems to think so."

The way he said it disconcerted her. She felt that he was naturally a serene and happy person and it was wrong that he should be bitter. Grace did not know what to say. She stood staring at him and wondered what his wife was like.

He met her eyes and at once looked down at the boxes of seedlings. "You'll be wanting the ground got ready for these," he said, "but flowers can wait. You're behindhand with the vegetable garden. Should have been dug and planted long ago."

"I know," she said humbly. "I've sown one row of peas and Martin, my old gardener, saw to the broad beans in November before he was ill, but not much else has been done."

"Beans doing fine and so are the lettuces," he said kindly. "Don't you worry. No one could expect an . . . a lady like you to dig all this."

She had been sure that he was going to say "old lady," and she was grateful that he had not. They were standing together outside the greenhouses. The last of the sunlight glowed on the red brick walls of the kitchen garden and turned his fair hair to gold.

"I'll make a start now," he said, moving away from her.

"But it's getting late, it's after seven."

"Be light enough for another hour, pity to waste it. I'll fetch my spade from the van."

In Her Garden

"There are spades and every tool you could want in that shed over there."

"I like using my own, if you don't mind."

"You'll be very late home. What will your wife say?"

He did not answer except by an almost imperceptible shrug.

Grace watched him walk away down the brick-paved path. When he had gone she shut the door of one of the greenhouses and went back to the house.

She wondered if she ought to ring up Hugh to make sure that he had really sent this man to her. She knew nothing of Ben Halden except what he had told her and that was little enough. Dilys had often warned her not to be too trusting. "Living alone as you do, you can't be too careful. There are such frightful people about and there are valuable things in the house," Dilys had said.

Grace hesitated, but only for a moment. Perhaps she was being credulous, but she did not think that Ben was anything except the simple, honest country-man he seemed. She would ring up Hugh later, to thank him for thinking of her, and after supper she would ring up Dilys too and tell her that the problem of the garden was solved.

It might be wiser though to wait a few days and see how Ben turned out; it was possible that he would be of little use. This she did not believe. Not only had he seemed willing, even eager, but when she had taken him round the garden he had shown himself knowledgeable and had made some useful suggestions. She would certainly ring up Dilys tonight.

How lucky I am, she thought, as she went to the kitchen to get her supper ready. Now I need not worry any more about the garden. I shall be able to enjoy it as I used to do. As she moved about the kitchen she kept an eye on the clock. An hour's daylight left, he had said. At eight she could go out onto the drive and wait by the van until he came. She must see him as nothing had been settled and he had not said when he would come again.

Although it was still light outside, it was growing dark in the kitchen and she switched on the light. As he was probably short of money, he might come to the back door to be paid for his hour. She listened for a knock which did not come, and at five to eight she took her purse from the dresser and hurried out to the drive.

The van was still there, gleaming whitely in the dusk. She had only a few minutes to wait before she heard him coming. He was whistling a gay, carefree little tune, high and sweet. It broke off when he saw her and his feet crunched on the gravel as he came up to her.

It was dark under the trees but here, on the drive, she could see his face. He was smiling.

"Made a good start?" she asked.

"Reckon so. Pity I had to stop."

"Tomorrow you can carry on where you left off. You will be here in the morning, won't you?"

He laid his spade in the back of the van before he answered, "If you want me to."

"Of course I do. Can you come every day? There's so much to be done."

"Can't come Wednesdays. Wouldn't do to let the doctor down."

"No, no, of course. But all the other days?"

He hesitated and then said slowly, "Should like to, anyway until I've got the place straight. Might take quite a while, you know. Could come expensive for you."

Her heart warmed to him. She said, "That's all right, I would give a lot to see my garden as it ought to be again. It's settled then. I'll see you in the morning."

"I'll be here soon after nine, if that suits you. Can't be earlier because I take the boy to school."

"Isn't there a school bus?"

"Yes, it calls at the Site. He's little though, and nervous-like. It's his first term and I'll take him to the door until he gets used to it. Well, I'll be off now. Good night."

He turned away and she cried, "Wait a minute! I owe you something for this evening—an hour, wasn't it?"

"No hurry about that. Tomorrow, or the end of the week will do."

"I'd rather settle up now." She held out the note to him.

As he took it from her, his fingers touched hers

and he exclaimed, "You're cold! You shouldn't be standing there without a coat. It's only just May, after all."

He sounded concerned and it was pleasant to know that there was still someone who cared if she were cold or not. Now that she came to think of it, she realized how chilled she was, and yet she felt an inner warmth, a glow that seemed to spread through her from her finger-tips. She said, a little breathlessly, "Yes, I'd better go in. Good night."

"Good night. See you tomorrow."

Grace heard the van start up as she closed the front door. The silent, empty hall confronted her. A wave of the loneliness she had denied to Dilys swept over her, but it soon went. "It's only just May," he had said. Long summer days lay ahead.

She went straight to the morning-room, lit the fire, and, going to the corner cupboard where she kept bottles and glasses, poured herself a drink; it would not do to catch cold now. As she pushed a chair up to the fire and sat, sipping her whisky and warming her hands, she knew that she was happier than she had been for a long time. It was really rather absurd to feel quite so elated because she had found a gardener.

When Mrs. Barrett came to work next morning there was a white van standing in the yard. Having parked the moped in the garage and hung her helmet on the handle-bars, she walked round the van, examining it carefully. I've seen you before, she said to herself. What are you doing here? A window was open and she looked inside; the van was empty except for some gardening tools. "I thought so," she said aloud, and hurried into the house.

Grace was finishing breakfast when Mrs. Barrett, still in her coat and scarf, put her head round the morning-room door and said, "There's a van parked in the yard."

"Yes, I know."

The little brown eyes, bright with curiosity, were fixed on her face. Grace enjoyed teasing Mrs. Barrett and she said nothing.

"Looks like that old van of Roper's, up at the shop."

In Her Garden

"Does it?"

Mrs. Barrett came into the room and shut the door. "They say Roper sold it cheap to that young Halden what married his wife's niece. Sorry for him, if you ask me."

Grace hadn't asked her, but now she said, "Take off your coat, Mrs. Barrett, fetch another cup and have some coffee. Why should Mr. Roper be sorry?"

Mrs. Barrett was surprised. This was not like the Mrs. Maitland she knew, but she did as she was told. When she sat down opposite Grace and took the proffered cup, she said, "That Sandra . . ."

"Sandra? You mean the niece, Halden's wife?"

"Yes, the Ropers brought her up, you know, after her parents died and she's her aunt all over again. Bess Roper is all honey if you keep on her right side, but she can be a proper menace. Nags her poor husband until he doesn't know where he is. Nothing he does is ever right."

Mrs. Barrett paused to drink her coffee, and Grace asked, "Is she pretty?"

"Who? Bess Roper?"

"No, the niece."

"You could say that, I suppose. She used to be. A taking little thing, all eyes. I can remember her fooling with the other girls at the bus stop on their way to school. Must be ten years ago—how time flies! She got a job in the town, keen to get away from her aunt, I expect. The next thing we heard was she had married, someone from the other side of the county."

"And now she's back?"

In Her Garden

"Yes, turned up again like a bad penny, husband, son, and all." Mrs. Barrett sniffed. "They're living in a caravan on the Site. That's a come-down for her. Her uncle gave her a job in the shop and she must have been glad to get it. Ben Halden's a pleasant-enough young chap in the pub, or so my Bert says, but he's not much good from all accounts. Been out of work for months, or so I've heard."

"He's working now," Grace said. "In my garden."

"Is he then? There now—I'd heard he was looking for a gardening job, I was going to tell you. Let's hope he's some use. How did you get hold of him?"

"Dr. Grainger sent him. He's working for the doctor too."

As Mrs. Barrett began to clear the table, Grace said, "I'll go down to the kitchen garden now and see how he's getting on. I'd better tell him to come up to the house at eleven for coffee."

"Tea would do. Martin always had tea. How long is he staying? Just the morning?"

"All day. What about his lunch?"

"He'll have brought something with him. A thermos, I expect, and sandwiches, if that wife of his could be bothered to make sandwiches. They say she doesn't exactly put herself out for him, or the boy for that matter. Leaves the child alone for hours, or so they say. I've heard that their caravan is little better than a pigsty. She was lazy as a girl, I remember, always in trouble with her aunt for thinking of nothing except clothes and a good time."

Mrs. Barrett added, "But then they'll say anything. Sandra was never popular as a girl and there's two sides to everything, isn't there? I shouldn't worry about Ben Halden if I was you."

"I worry about anyone who works for me, Mrs. Barrett," Grace said in the rather grand manner she could at times assume. "Have we any beer? It's going to be warm and beer might be better than coffee."

Not waiting for an answer, she hurried out into the garden. It was another radiant day, cool now but with a promise of heat to come. The lawn was wet with dew and her feet left dark prints in the shining grass; she should have changed her shoes. Grace had heard the van arrive a few minutes after nine and had half expected Ben to come to the kitchen door. He must have gone straight to work and she would find him digging where he had left off yesterday.

He was there, at the far end of the kitchen garden, his back turned to her. He could not have heard the wall door open for he did not look round. She stood still on the path and watched him. The sun was warm on her bare head and the scent of pear blossom, which seemed the very scent of spring, flowed over her.

His pullover hung on the espalier behind him and the blue T-shirt left his arms bare. He turned the heavy soil easily, rhythmically, moving with measured slowness as all real gardeners do; the newly dug ground grew steadily as she watched. He'll have it all cleaned and dug in no time, she thought. How lucky I am. She went slowly down the path and, when she was close, he straightened up and, leaning on his spade, turned to look at her.

In Her Garden

She said, "Good morning, Ben. How are you getting on? Another fine day."

"Yes, it looks set fair. Maybe we're in for a fine spell of weather at last."

"And before long we'll be thinking of watering?"

"Plenty of time for that," he said, and smiled. "I was thinking of getting some runners and peas in today, if you have the seeds. Too late for some things though. They'll have to wait for another year."

Another year. That had a pleasing, permanent sound. "I ordered packets and packets of seeds long ago," she said, "although how I thought I would get them all in, I don't know. They're in the greenhouse. Come along and I'll show you."

As Grace led the way, she saw that the greenhouse had already been opened, which was just as well as, for once, she had forgotten all about it, and the sun was growing hot. "You'll find all the seeds in this box," she told him, "and there are bean-poles and pea-sticks in the large shed. Let me know if you want anything else. I'll be in the house for a bit and then in the side garden, weeding."

He said, "Thank you," and at once turned away. He was at the door when she called after him, "Come up to the house at eleven for coffee. Mrs. Barrett will be in the kitchen. Go straight in."

She stayed a little longer alone in the greenhouse, turning over the packets of seeds without seeing them, her thoughts confused and vague. Then she carefully watered her boxes of seedlings and went back to the house.

In Her Garden

Towards the end of that first long, sunny day, Hugh came to see her. She was walking up and down the terrace, a cardigan over her shoulders, watching the evening shadows of the trees lengthen on the grass, when he appeared through the windows of the drawing-room. Grace was tired from her long hours working in the garden but, as always, she was glad to see him.

She liked Hugh Grainger. She liked his looks, his elegance, and his easy, nonchalant manners, and she liked his mind, which she found original and humorous, astringent. They had been close friends for many years and were at ease and happy in each other's company. He had first come to the village over twenty years ago as a junior partner to old Dr. Templer and had been content to stay and work here ever since. A specialist he had once sent her to had told her that Hugh was the best G.P. he had ever known and that he could have made a brilliant career for himself. Often she had upbraided him for his lack of ambition, called him incurably lazy, and he had cheerfully agreed. "I work hard when I have to, which is often," he said, "but I like a peaceful, easy, comfortable life and I have it here."

As he came towards her, she thought once again how handsome he was with his dark eyes and hair and his short, dark, now slightly grizzled beard. It pleased her that he was always well dressed, if in an easy, careless way. Dear Hugh, she thought, and held out her hands to him.

"The front door was open so I came straight in," he said as he took her hands in his and looked searchingly into her face. "This isn't a professional visit, but I can see that you are tired. I prescribe a chair indoors, as it's getting chilly, and a drink."

"It's such a lovely evening, I didn't want to miss it, but perhaps you're right." She looked up at him and said, "You're tired yourself, aren't you? Had a trying day?"

"Very trying. Sands is away and I had to take both surgeries. Half the village was there this evening. You would think that on a day like this they would forget their ills, but no."

"I'll get a drink for both of us. You can stay a little?"

"I'm going to, unless you want to have your supper."

"You know that I eat any time that suits me. What about you?"

"I told Mavis I might be late and not to wait. She's going out, some meeting or other."

As they went indoors, Grace asked, "How is Mavis?"

It was a routine question and received a routine answer. "Much as usual, very busy."

Grace had once thought that Hugh might marry Dilys and had never been able to decide if that would have pleased her or not. "You need not have worried," Hugh could have told her. "I liked Dilys then, I even found her attractive, but from the first it was you I came to see." Dilys had chosen to marry Desmond, that lean, sandy, silent, and shrewd man. Grace had been doubtful, he was so much older, for one thing, but the marriage had been a success. Dilys always seemed to do exactly as she liked, yet, when it came to something big, it was Desmond who ruled that roost. As for Hugh, he had married Mavis, something Grace would never understand.

Years ago, for his sake, she and Mavis had tried to find some common ground and failed. Now, as she poured him a drink in the morning-room, she thought once again what extraordinary women men choose to marry. Mavis was the best of wives and looked after Hugh and his delightful little house to perfection, but how dull she was! "Perhaps she is," Hugh could have said, "but I'm happy. I appreciate my Mavis, even if I often find your vagueness, your airy unpredictableness a refreshing relief." Grace wondered again what Ben Halden's wife was like. According to Mrs. Barrett she at least had been pretty. The only pretty thing about Mavis was her fair, wavy hair.

For the greater part of that morning in the garden Grace had resisted the impulse to go and see what Ben was doing. She had told herself that she must leave him to get on with his work in his own way and that he would resent interference. It was nearly time for luncheon before she went to the kitchen garden. He was in the greenhouse, eating the food he had brought with him; the thick, clumsy sandwiches looked as if he had made them himself. When she asked him if he had everything he needed, he did not stand up, as old Martin would have done. His voice was gentle, even deferential, as he answered, but he had no manners. This she noticed again when she gave him his afternoon tea in the kitchen. He sat stolidly at the table and let her wait on him, to pour out and refill the heavy kettle on the cooker and to fetch him a plate of biscuits as a matter of course, yet, from what she had heard from Mrs. Barrett, she doubted if his wife gave him such attention.

"Did your mother spoil you when you were a child?" she had asked him suddenly. He had looked up, taken aback. "My mother? Well, I reckon she did. I was the only one, like Peter," and he had added, "She's dead. Over ten years ago."

Grace seldom had tea in the afternoon, but she had fetched herself a cup and had sat down opposite him, resting her elbows on the table. He had fidgetted under her regard and had only relaxed when she fetched pencil and paper and began to make a list with him of seedlings he wanted for the garden. If I go slowly, he will soon be completely at ease with me, she had thought.

Hugh was speaking to her and she came back to the morning-room with a start.

"Ben Halden?" she said. "Yes, he's here."

"I really came to find out how he was getting on. You sounded enthusiastic when you rang up last night. How is he doing?"

"Very well. I'm so grateful to you for sending him to me. He says he's going to put the whole place in order and I think he will."

"He seems a pleasant chap, but I don't know much about him. I feel responsible in a way for wishing him on you."

"I'm glad you did."

"He needed work and you needed a gardener. I thought I was doing you both a favour."

"So you were. Then what's the trouble?"

"Nothing. I don't know why I feel uneasy. I suppose it's just because you're so vulnerable living here alone."

"Now you sound like Dilys. I'm surprised at you, Hugh. You've always encouraged me to stay on in this house."

"That's not because I think it's wise, it's just that I believe in people doing what they want to do."

Grace smiled at him. "And because you don't like seeing old people pushed around, you said that once."

"Old? Who's talking about being old? I thought we'd agreed that old age starts at eighty."

"So we did, and today I'm feeling younger than I have for some time, but we were talking about Ben Halden."

"Don't you find him difficult to talk to? I can hardly get a word out of him."

"I did at first. Now he's becoming quite loquacious."

"That's your sympathetic manner. You have a very

sympathetic manner, but only when you like. Mavis is terrified of you."

"Mavis! Of all people! I don't believe it."

"You can be rather grand and chilly, you know."

"I don't know and I doubt it."

He laughed. "Take my word for it then. You seem to have taken to Ben Halden anyway."

"For one thing he's such a terrific worker. Never seems to hurry, yet gets through an amazing amount in a short time."

"You said that he was still here. He's working late. It's after seven now."

"He told me that he likes to work until dark."

"Perhaps he's not particularly keen to get home, although I should have thought he would want to see his son before the child went to bed. I don't blame him though. His wife is a sour little thing, or so I thought."

Grace got up to refill his glass. "Tell me what you know about him," she said.

"Not much. He came to the surgery one evening. His boy was ill and he wanted me to come at once. He seemed worried so I went with him as soon as I could."

"They live in a caravan, I gather."

"Yes, on the Site. They had only just arrived."

"Mrs. Barrett says it's no better than a pigsty."

"That's a bit of an exaggeration, although it was rather untidy. I shouldn't think the girl is much of a manager."

In Her Garden

"What's she like?"

"Good looking, rather striking in a flimsy way. I didn't take to her. I disliked the contemptuous way she spoke to him in front of me. Should think they lead a cat and dog life and I'd say he might easily walk out on her if it wasn't for the boy."

"Was the child ill?"

"He was rather, some virus or other. He's a delicate child. I went again the next day. She wasn't there, works at the shop, Ben said. I gathered that he himself had been out of work for some time. He obviously doted on his son, couldn't do enough for him. A nice little fellow."

"Did you go again?"

"There was no need. Ben came to the surgery once again for a prescription. He kept on thanking me for what I'd done for his boy—you might think I had saved Peter's life. The next time I saw Ben was a few days ago when he drove up to the house in a van to ask if I knew anyone who wanted a gardener—he seemed to have a touching faith in me. I took him on for one day a week myself and gave him a list of names with yours at the top."

Grace went to the window. It was beginning to grow dark. Light still lingered on the stone of the terrace though the garden beyond was lost in shadow. She had not heard the van drive off, but Ben had probably gone home by now; they had agreed that she should pay him every Saturday so there had been no reason for him to come to the house. Tomorrow was

In Her Garden

Wednesday. She turned back to the room.

"So you see I know very little about him," Hugh was saying. "It's only a few weeks since they settled here. Still, we know already that he's a good worker. That's the important thing, isn't it?"

"Yes," Grace said. "I suppose it is."

They did not mention Ben Halden again for some time, but Hugh talked, as he loved to do, and Grace listened. Mavis, she suspected, was not very good at listening; she always had so much to do. His agile mind darted from subject to subject, going off at unexpected tangents, and sometimes it was difficult even for her to follow him. Often he made her laugh. This evening he regaled her with outrageous stories about poor Dr. Sands, his earnest, solemn, and conscientious young partner who got on his nerves. Hugh was, too, a terrific gossip, almost as bad as Mrs. Barrett, and sincerely interested in his village. He could be serious and he and Grace had much in common, the same rather unkind wit, the same taste in books and paintings, and would discuss what they had read and seen for hours. They had both managed to see the exhibition at Burlington House. Grace had gone up by an early train before lunching with Dilys, who would have wanted to see the exhibition with her. "Somehow I can *not* look at pictures with Dilys," she told Hugh.

"How is your own painting getting on?" he asked. "Done any lately?"

"Not much. There's never enough time and the

39

weather hasn't been kind. I did one thing though. It's not quite finished, but I'll show it to you if you like."

"Please do, then I really must go. It's time you had your supper."

In her youth Grace, having spent some time in art schools, had earned her living with botanical drawings. Her work had been exact and exquisite and had begun to be in demand. After years of marriage, when Dilys had gone to boarding-school, she had started to paint flowers in oils, often quite large canvases, always of flowers growing in her garden. These were painted with no exactness, being flower portraits in an almost abstract manner. She had had a small success; several had been exhibited and many had sold. Hubert had not been able to make head or tail of them, but Hugh had liked them well enough, although he was often critical.

Grace fetched a canvas from several stacked behind the sofa. Hubert had made her a fine studio in one of the attics, with the correct north light, but since he had died she always finished her pictures here, in the morning-room. "Why do I still call it that?" she had once asked Dilys, "when it is certainly my living-room. I eat here, work and rest here." It had been the morning-room, where the family had breakfasted when Hubert's mother and first wife were alive and the name had stayed.

"Pity the daylight has gone," she said, as she set the canvas up against the sofa cushions and switched on the standard lamp. "I'm quite pleased with this one."

Hugh crouched in front of the painting, studying it with his usual absorption. Then he looked up at her.

"I like this, I like the way you have the narcissi close up, white and gold and then diminishing in the distance into that blue haze."

"It's not finished, remember."

"I like it as it is, don't spoil it. I can almost smell them."

He stood up and put the canvas carefully back in its place.

"One good thing is that now Ben Halden is here, you'll have more time," he said. "I'd rather think of you painting in the garden than weeding, not to say digging."

"There will still be weeding to do. I can't expect one man to do everything."

"Of course not, this is too big a place. But don't overdo it. Pity you're such a perfectionist."

"You don't mean that, you're one yourself."

"Am I? Yes, I suppose I am."

As she helped him on with his coat, he said, "Well, let's hope that Ben goes on as well as he has begun."

"He goes to you tomorrow."

"So he does. You sound as if you regretted it. No, it's no use looking at me like that, Grace. I'm not going to be noble and say I'll do without him. I've a garden too, you know, and Mavis would not be pleased. Four whole days of Ben will have to be enough for you."

"Five. He's working on Saturdays."

"Then you're being greedy, Mrs. Maitland!"

She went with him into the hall. "Thanks for the drinks and talk, Grace," he said. "I feel refreshed."

"So do I," she assured him. "Good night, Hugh."

It was true. Hugh always did her good, and when he went left something of his vitality and good humour with her. She was smiling to herself as she went into the kitchen.

The smile faded. She said, aloud, "What shall I do all tomorrow?"

CHAPTER

3

Grace crossed the yard to the garages; there had been
a shower in the night and the cobbles were still wet
and shining in the sunlight. White pigeons rose into
the air and circled over the house as she started the
Mini.

It was a perfect day for gardening and there was no
knowing how long this fine weather would last. She
had planned the day's work at breakfast and then had
changed her mind; she felt restless, reluctant for once
to settle down to long hours alone in the garden. I
need a change, she had told herself, it's days since I
went out.

The countryside would be at its best with the apple
orchards in flower; she would drive the eight miles to
the Nurseries to fetch the seedlings she and Ben had
decided on yesterday. As she turned the Mini in the
yard, Mrs. Barrett ran out of the house waving a
piece of paper; they were out of butter and tea, which
meant a visit to the shop, something Grace avoided as

far as possible; it was always full of chattering women and she hated queueing. Every week she telephoned an order, which Mr. Roper delivered the next day, but she always forgot something. Bother, she thought, I'll do it on the way back.

At the bottom of the drive she turned left. The direct way skirted the village, yet she found herself driving round the Green and slowing down as she passed Hugh's house. Its Georgian front with shiningly clean sash windows, fanlight, and brass knocker rose almost from the pavement and nothing of the garden behind could be seen. The white van was parked in the roadway, but there was no sign of Ben.

For a moment she toyed with the idea of calling on Mavis, but Mavis, who did all her own housework, with one morning's assistance from Mrs. Barrett, and was fanatically house proud, would hardly welcome a visitor at ten in the morning. Grace drove on past the King's Arms and through the village. She was annoyed with herself for being so foolish and coming so far out of her way; it was a day for open countryside and not for buildings, however picturesque. She was fond, though, of the village, which, compared with so many, was unspoiled. It still had its own school, vicar, and flourishing village shop, was still a close-knit community where almost everyone knew everyone else. When she left the last houses behind and was out in the woods and green fields, she wound the car window down as far as it would go. The fresh May air flowed over her and lifted her short, fine hair. The orchards began and on each side there was now a sea of white and pink. Poor Dilys, she thought, living in London. Poor everyone who was not abroad on this morning in Kent.

The Nurseries were reached all too soon and there she spent a happy time exploring the long glasshouses, breathing the warm, damp green earthy smell, and talking to Tucker, the foreman, an old friend who was never too busy when she appeared. Together they loaded the boxes of seedlings into the Mini, including some extra annuals. She had meant to plant very few annuals this year, but now that she had Ben, she felt she could indulge herself. Grace drove away at last, her cheeks pink with exertion and pleasure, feeling pleased with all the world.

There was still plenty of time before luncheon and, having forgotten her shopping, she took a longer way back that would bring her out on the side of the village nearest to her house. On the way she passed the caravan site. Grace had never paused before to inspect the Site, which had caused such an uproar among the more conservative inhabitants of the village. She parked at the entrance and got out. The Site was larger than she had imagined. The caravans, of many shapes and sizes, stood in orderly rows. Most had television aerials, some had cars parked beside them, and one or two had deck-chairs set out near their steps; children played on the worn grass; washing fluttered.

Grace advanced slowly. She had no real reason to

be there and she felt conspicuous and out of place. From one large caravan she passed came the sound of voices and the smell of cooking, but most looked closed and empty, their occupants probably out at work. She saw a long-haired young woman with a perambulator beside her hanging washing on a line and went up to her. "Can you tell me which is the Haldens' caravan?" she asked. Having come as far as this, she was determined to see for herself where Ben lived.

The girl looked at her suspiciously, her glance going over Grace from her untidy hair, the short scarlet jacket and dark trousers to her rather muddy shoes.

"Second on the left, this row," she said, jerking her head in that direction. "They're most likely out. His van's not there and she's usually up at the shop mornings."

The shop! Grace looked at her watch. The shop shut at one—there was still time. "Thank you," she said. "Now that I'm here, I'll make sure." She smiled at the girl, who did not smile back. The baby in the pram began to cry and Grace retreated.

Although she knew that she was being watched, she went to the second caravan on the left and knocked at the door. When no one answered, she turned the handle; the door was locked. The caravan was not as large nor as opulent as some of its neighbours and it had no aerial. Faded curtains were drawn across the windows. A child's toy engine lay on the steps.

As Grace went back to the car, avoiding the young

woman with the baby, she wished that she had not come. The Site depressed her; it seemed sad that any-one should live there. She had heard that there was a long waiting-list for a council house. Poor Ben.

It was a quarter to one when she reached the shop, but it was still crowded. She took her basket and found what she wanted on the shelves. As she joined the queue at the counter, she looked round and won-dered which of the three girls moving in their blue overalls among the customers was Ben's wife; she only knew one by sight and the other two were both dark-haired. Mrs. Roper was behind the counter, ringing the cash register, talking incessantly. When she saw Grace, she called out in her loud, slightly insolent voice, "Good morning, Mrs. Maitland. Haven't seen you for ages. Been keeping well?"

As Grace replied, she saw the nearest girl lift her head and turn to look at her. Their eyes met across the width of the shop. She was smaller, much slight-er, than her aunt, with the same black hair and eyes and dead white skin. Grace did not like Mrs. Roper, and she did not think that she liked this girl, which was absurd because she knew nothing about her, ex-cept what Mrs. Barrett had said. For a moment she wondered if she should speak to Ben's wife, begin perhaps, "Your husband works for me," but the girl turned her back before Grace could move. She won-dered why there had been a look of hostility in those large, but oddly opaque black eyes. She was sure that she had not imagined it.

CHAPTER

4

The fine weather held all through the next three weeks. Grace could not remember such a radiant May. The days were warm, the nights cool, sometimes with a light shower, which was all that was needed to freshen the garden. The blossom was at its best: apple and pear and hawthorn. It seemed to her that the whole countryside was rejoicing in the coming of summer.

Order and well-being were slowly returning to Setons' garden. It was a pleasure now to walk in the kitchen garden in the evenings and to look at the neat rows of growing plants. Grace spent long hours planting out her flower seedlings and weeding, but the sense of pressure had gone. There was time, she now felt, to start another painting, and for all she wanted to do.

There was no interruption to the even flow of her days. Dilys and Desmond were on holiday in Greece. Grace seldom left the house and garden and avoided going to the village. She tried to put the visit she had made to the Site out of her mind; the thought of the caravan distressed her, as did the remembrance of that malevolent look she had met in the shop. Sometimes in the evenings when she was tired, she saw those hostile eyes again and a shadow, as if from a passing cloud, touched the brightness of her day. In the afternoons she gave Ben his tea in the kitchen; they would sit on opposite sides of the table in the window that looked out at the cobbled yard with its pigeons, and while they drank their tea would talk, not as she and Hugh talked, but in a slower, more peaceful, and desultory way, with long pauses.

Ben never mentioned his wife. He talked not only of the garden, but of things he had read in the paper, or heard discussed in the pub, asking her opinion and listening gravely to her answers. Most of all, he talked of his son. Grace was indulgent and sympathetic, but she was beginning to be rather tired of Peter and his doings, and would try gently to lead Ben to talk of something else. They did not always agree and would have quite fierce arguments as they had done over the sweet peas. She had wanted peasticks and Ben canes. "I don't want huge flowers on long stalks," she had told him. "I want a close hedge of colour." He had been obstinate, had argued, and, exasperated, she had almost said, "Well, it's *my* garden," the last thing she wanted to say. When she had realized that his heart was set on the summer flower show, that he had visions of enormous sweet peas and first prizes, she had compromised, saying, "We will have two rows, one with canes and one with pea-sticks." His face had lightened at once and he had said, admiringly, "Just like you to think of that."

There had been another argument over what he was to call her. "Mrs. Maitland is so stiff and formal," she had said.

"It's the proper name to call you by."

"Perhaps it is, but I don't like it."

"What then? Would you rather I called you Madam? I will if you like."

"No. I don't like that either—makes me feel I'm in a shop. What about Mrs. Grace?"

He was shocked. "That wouldn't do at all," he cried and flushed scarlet, as he so easily did. After a moment he looked across the table at her, smiled, and said, "Tell you what, I'll call you Ma'am. That's what they call the Queen. No one can say 'Your Majesty' all the time." He said it solemnly, but his eyes had a twinkle in them, and she laughed.

Their afternoon sessions always ended the same way. Ben would look at his watch, a watch she had given him when she had discovered that he had to come up to the house when he wanted to know the time. He had been reluctant to take it. "Kind of you," he had said, "but no."

"Why not?"

"It's too good for one thing, must have cost a packet."

"It didn't cost me anything. It belonged to my

husband. Do take it, Ben. You can consider it lent if you like."

Having looked at his watch, he would get to his feet awkwardly and say, "Well, I'd better be off, plenty to do. Thanks for the tea." She would hear him whistling as he crossed the yard.

For Grace the busy, peaceful days, almost without a care, went by too quickly, became warmer and longer, and it was June.

CHAPTER

5

One morning towards the middle of the month, Grace stood in the yard looking up at the row of windows above the garage. Long ago, before the war, Hubert had converted the loft over what had once been stables and coach house into a flat, first for a chauffeur and later for a married couple who had worked for a short time as cook and gardener. It had been empty for many years.

Grace had been planting begonias in the tubs under the kitchen windows and her trowel was still in her hand. Why didn't I think of that before? she asked herself. Of course, it's the perfect answer.

Not waiting to take off her gloves, she hurried past the greenhouses into the kitchen garden to look for Ben. He was not there, nor was he anywhere near the house. She stood on the top of the steps looking over the rose garden. The last week had been cooler, with some cloud and wind; she had thought the spell of fine weather was over, but today it was back and looked as if it had come to stay. The sun was hot and there was only a gentle breeze that barely moved the leaves; the roses were fully out and their scent came to her where she stood above them.

Where was Ben? Usually he was easily traced; she had only to follow the sound of his whistle, which reminded her of a blackbird's song. Today, as she listened, she only heard the whirr of a mower. Of course—he was in the orchard, cutting the long grass as he had told her only that morning he intended to do.

Grace hurried down the steps and through the gap in the yew hedge to her right, rehearsing in her mind what she meant to say. "I've had a wonderful idea, Ben," she would begin.

He was at the far end of the orchard where the side gate, seldom used, opened on to the road. He did not see her at once, and she was close before he looked up and switched the mower off. The long grass lay in swaths, its warm grass smell lost for the moment in the fumes of the exhaust. He was bare to the waist and the leaf shadows of the apple trees patterned his fair, gleaming skin. One lock of hair hung over his eyes, and this he put back with a brown hand as he looked at her enquiringly.

"I've had a wonderful idea, Ben," she said. "Listen . . ."

Ben smiled then, and reached for his shirt, which hung from a branch. He pulled it on over his head and listened gravely, his face becoming expressionless as she talked. When she finished, rather abruptly, put off by his lack of response, all he said was, "No!"

It was said loudly, almost violently, and after a moment he added, more gently, "Thanks all the same, but it wouldn't do."

"Why not, Ben?" She was surprised and annoyed. "As I said, it's quite a roomy little flat, much better surely than a caravan? There's a bedroom, a kitchen, a sitting-room, and a little room that would do for Peter. I've got more furniture than I know what to do with, I could make it comfortable for you. Then Peter could have a kitten, or even a dog, which are not allowed on the Site, he would like that, wouldn't he? And there always used to be a stable cat about the yard."

He said nothing, and she went on, refusing to be discouraged, "Then think of the time and petrol you would save."

Ben shook his head.

"Don't you think you ought to ask your wife?"

"No, I don't."

Grace knew that it was no use persisting. She said, "Why, Ben? Can't you at least tell me why?"

He looked at her dumbly, shook his head again, and at last said, "I like it here. It would spoil it. There wouldn't be anywhere."

"Wouldn't be anywhere? What do you mean?"

After a long pause he added, "There would be no-where. You don't know."

She waited, hoping there was more to come. Ben

looked down at the grass and did not meet her eyes
again. She saw that he was silently asking her if he
might get back to work, only waiting for her to go,
and presently she went away.

It became very hot and dry, as in fine summers it
sometimes does in June. Sprinklers were out on the
lawns, hoses unrolled. Ben brought the first strawberries and early peas up to the house. Grace wore linen
trousers or the lightest of blue cotton dresses, and
Ben, ceasing to be shy, respectful, or old-fashionedly
prudish, whichever he had been in her presence, went
everywhere half-naked and was soon as brown as a nut.

He now came to work early in the mornings, almost as soon as the sun was up. Grace was sure that
he was glad to be out of that stuffy caravan, but all
he would say was "I like early mornings, not many
do, so I have everything to myself."

"You see the countryside as it ought to be then,"
she agreed.

"Yes, and the creatures are still out and about. I
saw a fox today, crossing the road. It's quiet, too, no
cars or radios. This morning there was a donkey
braying, an awful ugly sound, but real country, not
like a tractor working."

"What about Peter?" she asked. "How does he
manage over school?"

"He goes on the bus with the others. He's used to
school now, says he quite likes it."

In Her Garden

"How does he get home? By bus again?"

"No, the little ones leave earlier. His mother picks him up. Mrs. Roper lets her off round three and she takes him home on her bike. It all fits in, Peter is all right."

"I'm sure he is. You would see to that."

"I would, and I do." He said it grimly, and he added, "Sometimes I nip off home round about five for half an hour to see him having his tea. You don't mind, do you? You'd hardly notice I was gone."

"Of course I don't mind," Grace exclaimed. "You work hard enough."

Grace was worried that Ben should put in such long hours; he never left in the evenings before eight, and sometimes later. When she said as much to him, he assured her that he took at least a couple of hours off in the heat of the day. "Much better to have a rest in the open after my dinner than to sleep mornings in the caravan," he told her. She came upon him once lying fast asleep under a tree in the orchard, his head pillowed on his arm, his mouth a little open. She had been resting too, in her chair on the terrace but, unable to sleep and bored with her book, had wandered through the garden, driven by a restlessness that often came upon her these days and prevented her from sleeping as she should at nights. It's the heat, she had told herself, it's only natural. Ben had not woken when she stood looking down at him, and, feeling an intruder, someone who had blundered in where she was not meant to go, she had gone as quietly as she could across the orchard and back to the terrace.

In Her Garden

Dilys came down the next day, having telephoned at breakfast. It was nearly six weeks since she had last come. Grace had put her off the week before, ostensibly because of the grey weather; the truth was that she did not want to be disturbed. There was no getting out of it this time, and of course she would be glad to see Dilys, of whom she was very fond, and all would be well and pleasant as long as they did not start the usual argument. "I'm longing to see your paragon of a gardener," Dilys had said.

Grace made what preparations she could in the time, cutting roses from those beds that were in the shade and making the best luncheon she could. Luckily there was most of a roast chicken left and this she made into a chicken aspic. Ben brought up a lettuce, new potatoes and strawberries and the last of the asparagus, and Mrs. Barrett volunteered to go on her moped to the village for cream. Dilys will be pleased, Grace said to herself as she put a bottle of white wine into the refrigerator. She's greedy and that's a luncheon fit for anyone. No one could say that I haven't taken trouble this time.

When the car drove up she went out onto the drive to meet it. Dilys greeted her with affection and was in a good humour, although she looked hot and complained once again of the traffic. "It's too hot a day to be shut in a stuffy car in a traffic jam," she said as they went into the house. "I won't go back until this evening, if that's all right by you, Mother."

Grace said that it was and, while Dilys went upstairs to wash, and then to the kitchen to have a word with Mrs. Barrett, she carried a tray of drinks out to the terrace, where she had already arranged a table and comfortable chairs. This must be a happy, peaceful day, she told herself. No disagreements if I can help it.

The lightest of breezes was blowing on the terrace and it was pleasantly cool out of the sun. When Dilys appeared, they sat together talking companionably. Dilys had plenty to tell of the holiday in Greece. "You should have come with us, Mother," she said. "It would have done you good to get away for a bit."

"It was kind of you and Desmond to suggest it, but there was too much to do in the garden, for one thing."

"You and your garden! Do you ever think of anything else?"

"Quite often."

"Your paintings perhaps, but they are almost extensions of the garden, aren't they?"

Grace looked at her stepdaughter, surprised at this perception. "I suppose they are, in a way," she said slowly. "You should be glad that I have the garden, Dilys. I might be lonely without it."

"You needn't be lonely even for a moment if you don't want to be. You could . . ."

"Oh, don't let's start that again," Grace exclaimed. "Not today. I want today to be perfect."

Dilys was touched. She put her hand on Grace's arm and said, "It will be, I'm going to enjoy every minute. Who could help it on such a lovely day. Tell me about this Ben Halden. Is he still a success?"

"He is indeed. Wait until you see what he has done in the kitchen garden. I didn't know anyone worked like that nowadays. He's often here before seven and stays until after eight, sometimes later."

"Good Heavens! It must cost you a fortune."

"Soon after he came, we arranged that I should give him a weekly wage, and he won't take any more. It's a good wage, but he looks after the Mini for me and saves me expense as he does all the mowing. I bought him one of those big mowers you sit on."

"That must have cost something!"

"It did, but it will pay for itself in time. He will do the hedges too eventually. And it's not that long, Dilys. He takes two or three hours off in the middle of the day."

"I suppose he goes home then."

"No, he rests here, either in the orchard or the greenhouses."

"Is he married?"

"Yes."

"Then I'm sorry for his wife."

"You needn't be. She is out much of the day herself, works in the shop. Anyway, they don't get on. They live in one of those caravans and Mrs. Barrett says she gives him an awful life."

"Mrs. Barrett would."

"Apparently all the village knows it. Hugh doesn't like her, or the way she speaks to her husband."

"What has Hugh to do with it?"

59

In Her Garden

"Ben's son was ill . . ."

"So he has a child. You don't talk about him as if he were a family man."

"Don't I?"

Grace got up to get Dilys another drink. She thought, Although Ben has a son, he's no family man. He seems to me to be a lonely person. If he's at home anywhere, it's here. To Dilys she said, "Shall we have a look round the garden before luncheon? There's plenty of time."

Dilys admired the roses, which were at their best, and when they made their leisurely way across the newly mown lawns, she said, "The place looks very different already. I'm beginning to think this Ben of yours is all you say. Where is he?"

Ben was hoeing in the kitchen garden. He stopped work as they approached and, to Grace's annoyance, retreated into the greenhouses. It was only to put on his shirt and he reappeared almost at once. He did not smile when she said, "This is Mrs. Fenton, Ben. She's come down for the day from London. It's six weeks since she was here and I want her to see what you have done."

"Good morning, Ben," Dilys said. "What an improvement! Now it looks like a kitchen garden again. You've done wonders."

What else could Dilys have said? There was nothing wrong with the words, it was the way she said them, far too heartily, with a touch of condescension. Perhaps he did not like being called Ben by a stranger. What should Dilys have called him? Halden?

60

In Her Garden

That would have been fatal. Mr. Halden? Perhaps, but that seemed rather absurd.

Grace sighed. She saw that this encounter was not going to be a success. Ben's face had taken on its wooden expression and he looked almost surly. Dilys, who always had the best of intentions, often rubbed people the wrong way; it was a form of insensitiveness, Grace had decided. How strange though that in a few minutes, with only a few words said—Ben had not even spoken—there should be antagonism between them. Grace could feel it in the air.

"Is there anything we can give Mrs. Fenton to take back this evening, Ben?" she said. "What about some broad beans? The strawberries have only just started, Dilys, and what there are we're having for luncheon. Next time you come we'll send you away laden. Now we're rather behindhand."

Ben muttered something about lettuces. "See what you can find, please, and bring a basket up to the house when you come in for tea. I'll pick some roses later." Grace spoke more curtly than she usually did to Ben. She was annoyed with him and, for that matter, with Dilys. There was now a slight shadow on the day that she had hoped would be so bright.

"The sun is too hot," she said to Dilys. "Let's go back to the house. It's time for luncheon anyway."

"So that is Ben Halden," Dilys said as they crossed the yard to the back-door. "He's not what I expected. From what you said, I thought he would be better looking and not so shy and awkward."

"I never told you he was good-looking."

"Didn't you? Well, you must have implied it. I was expecting an Adonis, not a rather ordinary, surly young man."

"Ben isn't surly." Grace spoke hotly and then checked herself. "You're laughing at me, Dilys," she said.

"Not laughing, only teasing. What does it matter if he is good looking or not? He's evidently a good gardener, as I told him. That didn't go down very well, did it? What more could I have said?"

Grace did not answer and neither Ben nor the garden was mentioned again until lunch was nearly over. Then Dilys said, "When are you coming to us for a few days? You always do in June."

"I couldn't possibly leave now."

"Why not? Now that you have Ben, you can't pretend that the garden couldn't do without you. I'm sure you need a change. You are thinner than ever and you seem very nervy, on edge."

"That's the heat."

"London can be very pleasant in June. You said so yourself."

"Not when it's as hot as this. No, Dilys. Ask me again in winter. I should like to come then."

"I want you to come now. I don't see much of you, but you won't, I suppose. You never think of me."

Grace was irritated to see that there were tears in Dilys's eyes. It was strange that such a seemingly calm and statuesque woman should dissolve into tears so easily. She said sharply, "There's no need to cry,

Dilys. Stop it, please," and added, more gently, "Summer will be over only too soon. It's kind of you to ask me, but I don't want to go away now."

The drowsy afternoon passed slowly. Again Grace could not rest; she had slept for a short time in her long chair, but now was wide awake. Everyone else was asleep, she was sure, in the still and silent garden, Ben under the trees in the orchard, Dilys in a hammock slung in the shade. She and Dilys had agreed to meet for tea at four and Dilys would start back for London soon after six. "I meant to stay longer," Dilys had said, "but I ought to get back to give Desmond his dinner. He will have had a long hot day, poor man." Grace had not urged Dilys to stay.

She got up and went into the kitchen and set about getting tea ready, a trolley to be wheeled into the morning-room where she had opened the windows wide on to the terrace and Ben's tea to be laid on the kitchen table. When all was ready, she found pencil and paper and wrote a note for Ben, which she propped against his tea-pot: "Please make yourself tea. I have put everything ready." After hesitating a moment, she wrote: "Sorry to miss our usual talk."

It was only half-past three. She lingered in the kitchen for a few minutes, listening to the cooing of the pigeons in the yard before she went back to the terrace to wait for Dilys.

The next day was even warmer, too hot and sultry for comfort. There was no breeze at all and by midday Hubert's thermometer in the hall had risen into the eighties. Ben declared that it would not last, that there would be thunder before the day was out.

The heat did not seem to affect him. He worked as usual, but Grace found it too hot in the garden. She tried to write letters in the morning-room; she got out her unfinished painting and put it back again. She could not settle to anything and wandered round the house and, standing at the windows, looked out at the sun-drenched lawns, or up at the sky for a sign of a cloud. The sky remained an unrelieved blue, but it seemed to her that there was a menace on the heavy air, that something momentous was lurking just below the horizon. What is the matter with me? she asked herself and, going back to the morning-room, sat down at her writing-table and resolutely picked up her pen.

In Her Garden

In the night she had heard, over and over again, Dilys saying, "You never think of me." That was not quite true, but true enough to make her conscience-stricken, as Dilys often made her feel. Lying awake, she had remembered Hubert saying to her long ago when Dilys was thirteen, an awkward, unattractive age, "Can't you show more interest in the child? Can't you be kinder? She's so fond of you." Grace had been indignant, she remembered, and had protested that she was always thinking of Dilys and did everything possible for her. "I'm sure you do, my dear," he had said, "but what she needs from you is a little warmth, love." Grace had felt guilty then, as she had felt last night. What can I do, she asked herself? She could not bear to leave the garden, but she could write to Dilys and ask her and Desmond to come down and stay with her for as long as they liked.

When the letter was written she sat still, looking down at it. It was no good. She did not want them here. She did not want anyone, and Desmond, at least, would not want to come. He liked to spend any free time he had at his seaside cottage, sailing his beloved boat. With a sigh of relief, she tore up the letter.

Although the kitchen was in the cooler side of the house it was stiflingly hot. From her place at the table in the window Grace could see, beyond the pots of geraniums on the sill, the sun haze dancing on the cobbles of the yard. Two flies buzzed lazily against the ceiling, round and round, and the warm, pungent smell of geranium was heavy on the air.

She drank her iced coffee slowly and looked across the table at Ben. It was too hot for much talk and they sat in companionable silence. His elbows were on the table and his cup in both hands; he smiled his slow, lazy smile as his blue eyes met hers. He had preferred his usual tea and the hot strong stuff had brought beads of sweat out on his upper lip and forehead. His brown arms, covered with fine, pale, shimmering hairs, were bare. As if in a dream, Grace stretched out her hand to touch, to stroke them, and snatched it back again when Ben put his cup down and, turning his head towards the window, said, "Listen! Is that thunder?"

Grace could not speak. She sat with bent head, looking down at the table. For the rest of her life the smell of geraniums would bring back this moment. She forced herself to pick up her glass and she, too, heard the thunder.

"It's nearer," Ben said. "We'll catch it before long, and a good thing too. We need rain, and a storm will clear the air."

"Yes, it will," she agreed. Her voice sounded unnatural, strained, and she felt him look at her.

"You all right?" he asked. "You've gone very pale."

She looked at him then and the concern in his eyes almost undid her. He was kind, he was fond of her, she was sure. He would understand . . . Don't be idiotic, she told herself fiercely. At the first hint of any such thing he would run a mile.

"It's nothing," she said. "I've a headache, that's all. The thunder . . ."

"It's terrible close. Why not rest for a bit, lie down?"

"I think I will. I'll go upstairs."

"You do that," Ben said, as she stood up. "I'll clear the tea, leave it to me, and then I'd better see to the greenhouses. We don't want them flooded out."

At the door, Grace looked back. He was still sitting at the table finishing his tea, in his slow deliberate way. He was silhouetted against the light and she could not see his face. There was no need. She knew now that she knew him by heart.

The storm broke soon after six. Grace, from the landing window, had watched thunder clouds roll up from below the horizon and spread across the sky, extinguishing the sunlight and darkening the world. It was true that she had a headache, but she had not lain down in her bedroom. Instead she sat on the deep window-seat looking out over the garden and tried to collect her thoughts.

The wind came first, bending the tree-tops and sending a scurry of dust and leaves whirling across the lawns, which had turned a strange livid green. It was followed by the rain, sheets of driving rain that blotted out the garden and streamed down the windowpanes.

It was cruel that this strange thing, as violent as the storm, should happen to her when there could be no hope of happiness, only yearning and frustration. She had never fallen in love easily, even as a girl, and now at her age—how ridiculous, how painful! Why now? she asked herself, and why Ben? Why not her dear Hugh, who was a little nearer her own age and was her own kind? There was no answer and never could be. Love can happen for no reason and at any time, a flash of lightning out of the blue. We do not change. Within our ageing bodies we are the selves we have always been.

The sensible thing to do would be to send Ben away. Grace knew that she would never have the strength to do it, and it would be hard on him. He has done nothing wrong, she thought. I must hope this, this infatuation—I must not call it anything else—will not last, that I will come to myself one day and see him as the ordinary, simple young man he is. Meanwhile, I must accept it and go on as if nothing had changed. "As long as no one," she whispered, "especially not Ben, please God, even suspects, I can bear it."

The storm did not last long. The rain lessened and ceased. The clouds broke and moved away, and over the rose garden a rift of blue appeared. Grace opened the window and leaned out. The whole garden sparkled with moisture as the sun shone again; the scent of newly soaked earth came up to her.

The roses would be dashed and spoiled, but some of them would recover and there would be other roses. Grace decided to go out and see how the garden had fared. She would not look for Ben, nor would she avoid him. If she came across him and he asked how she was, she would tell him that her headache had gone and she felt better.

Grace was in the morning-room writing a letter, as
she often was in the weeks that followed the storm.
The fine, warm weather went on and on without another break and, as she wrote, the scents of high summer came to her through the open window, yet she
seldom looked up. The words, in her large, sloping
handwriting, flowed across the pages. Each time
when she had finished, she would fold her letter
without reading it through and put it in a small rosewood box that had once been her mother-in-law's
workbox. Before leaving the room, she would lock
the box and hide it in the bottom drawer of the bureau where she kept her important papers.

There were several letters in the box. They all began, "My dearest Ben," and all were signed, "Grace."
The first had been written a few days after the storm.

My dearest Ben,
I have decided to write to you whenever I feel
I must, when I can bear it alone no longer.

In Her Garden

These letters will be safety-valves for in them I will write without thought or inhibition, pouring it all out because no one will ever read them. I have found a small, strong box with a key. I will keep my letters in it for a while and then I will destroy them.

I meant to let myself go but when it comes to it, I find there are some things I can't bring myself to write, so I will write to you with restraint as I would do if you were really going to read my letters. I would not want to make you blush, as you so easily do. I will keep my more lurid imaginings for the nights, which are very long and very lonely. Old women should not have such feelings. Why old women and not old men? The world may smile but it does not think the worse of an old man who falls in love with a young girl, no one is disturbed or disgusted. How very unfair, but when was life ever fair?

To me it doesn't make a jot of difference that I'm old enough to be your mother—no, your grandmother! I do not feel towards you as I would towards a son, far from it. I am a woman of no particular age, most painfully and uselessly in love.

I am not wholly unhappy. Deep down, there is a flicker of joy that will not be denied. I suppose it's something to be able to feel so much again. The quality of life has changed. Its colours have become more vivid. I am more alive than I have been for years.

In Her Garden

Some of the letters were several pages long, others only a few lines.

My dearest Ben,

I hate Wednesdays. On Wednesdays I can't settle to anything. I try to avoid Mrs. Barrett for fear that she will see something is wrong, and I wander round the garden doing nothing. I can't even write to you.

Dearest Ben,

When one loves one wants to give and give. If I were young I could give myself but that being out of the question, I would like to heap presents on you. I can't do that either, the watch was as far as I dared to go. What can I do for you? I only want to do you good, to make your life easier and secure. That is why I leapt at the chance when Mrs. Barrett told me about the van.

I wonder why Mrs. Roper is making trouble now. Does she just like to make trouble? According to Mrs. Barrett she went for your wife in the shop in front of everyone, saying that Roper was a soft old fool to let you have the van at such a price and for you to pay back only five pounds a week was ridiculous. She said you didn't always do even that and they couldn't afford to have good money tied up that way. "I bet Sandra took it out of Ben when he got home," Mrs. Barrett said. Apparently in the shop your wife didn't answer Mrs. Roper back. "We were all waiting to hear her stick up for her husband, but she didn't say a word," Mrs. Barrett said, "just stood there with such a look on her face. Gave me quite a turn."

Mrs. Barrett has a vivid way of expressing herself. I could see that white face, which was why I rushed straight off to find you. You didn't want to tell me what you had agreed to pay for the van. Perhaps you thought it was none of my business. It was though. Anything that concerns you concerns me. Three hundred, you at last said, of which you had managed to pay back a bit, although there had been a week or two when you couldn't manage it. I didn't have much money in the house, so I got the Mini out and drove off to town to the bank.

You hated to take it from me, didn't you? You went scarlet and put your hands behind your back, as Peter might have done, when I held the envelope out to you. It took all my powers of persuasion before you saw reason. I wonder if you would always give in to me eventually. Am I the stronger?

When I argued that Mr. Roper probably needed the money more than I did, that you could pay me back as it suited you without worry, you said, "It's not him, he'd never, it's her. She's a proper bitch, that one." You said it with such bitterness that it upset me. Bitterness doesn't belong to you. It was when I asked if you wanted Mrs. Roper to harry your wife again in public that you gave in. Perhaps the thought of another scene in that caravan was too much for you, poor Ben. I hate to think of that bad-tempered little chit railing at you. Mrs. Barrett knows someone who has a caravan not far from yours, and she says that at times your wife's voice can be heard all over the Site. I used not to listen to Mrs. Barrett's gossip. Now I do. I ought to be ashamed of myself.

That night I went to bed almost happy. At last I had done something positive for you.

Dearest Ben,

Has there ever been such a summer, so fine, so warm, so radiant? The golden days go on and on, it's like a dream. I resent any interruption.

Dilys is annoyed with me because I wouldn't go to London and has kept away, but Hugh came to see me yesterday evening, the first time for weeks as he and Mavis have been on holiday; in a way I was glad to see him. It was quite late. You had gone home, a little earlier than usual. I had heard the van drive off as I ate my supper. That is always a bad time for me. When I know you are no longer anywhere near I feel desolate, which was why Hugh was welcome.

We sat on the terrace in the last light until the midges drove us in. I made him coffee as he didn't want a drink. We talked as usual, or I thought we did. He is too acute though. He said suddenly, "Where are you, Grace? You're miles away." That brought me up with a jerk. I had been listening to him, but at the same time I was thinking about you. I must be more careful.

Is my control wearing thin? It is tiring to keep such strong feelings to myself. Sometimes I wonder if you have guessed, you are always so kind and gentle to me. Then I am sure that such an idea has never entered your head. You wouldn't stay if it had, or would you? It would be against your own interests to go. Am I beginning to doubt even you? The strain must be beginning to tell. I almost told Hugh, the words were on my lips as I looked up and saw him watching me. Instead I told him about the van.

To my surprise he was quite cross. We had one of our small quarrels. He said that it was wrong to have put you under such an obligation to me, and what would the village think? I don't see why anyone should know. I asked you not to tell Mr. Roper where you got the money. Hugh smiled pityingly when I said this and assured me that everyone in the village always knew everything, and where else could you have got it? When I told him that the money was only lent, that you would pay it back, he said, "I wonder." That made me furious.

He was right about one thing. The village at

least knows that you gave Mr. Roper the money. "The whole of it, in one go," Mrs. Barrett told me all about it. "Where do you suppose Ben got hold of it?" she asked, watching my face. "Perhaps a win on the Pools?" I suggested, and she laughed.

Hugh and I parted amicably. I soothed him down. I can't afford to lose such a friend, even for you.

Dearest Ben,

An odd thing happened today in the garden. Your wife has been here. I saw her. She was standing absolutely still watching me. It was Wednesday again and I was in the rose garden, cutting off the dead heads. Something made me look round, and there she was in the gap in the yew hedge. She gave me a shock. There was something so intent in her stillness and the way she stared at me. I thought she was trying to make up her mind to speak to me and all I could do was to stare back but, after a moment, I took a step towards her and tried to smile. She was off in a flash and when I reached the hedge, I saw her running through the orchard towards the side gate. She was wearing a yellow dress.

On a Wednesday afternoon the shop would be shut, but surely she should be fetching Peter from school? I suppose she chose a Wednesday because she knew you wouldn't be here. I shan't tell you she came. You have enough to trouble you as it is.

What did she want? Had she come out of curiosity to see me and the garden; if so, why should she look at me with such venom? No one, not even Hugh, has guessed my secret, but I begin to wonder if she has. I have often thought that wives possess a sixth sense where their husbands and other women are concerned that scents danger, however unlikely, and often before it occurs! I should feel flattered but surely she could not be jealous of an old woman like me? Of one thing I am certain. She is still in love with you. I feel almost sorry for her.

Dearest Ben,

The school holidays have started and now you bring Peter here with you. You asked my permission and of course I said, "Yes." I wonder what would have happened if I had said no. I think that his mother should have taken time off from the shop to look after him. I said as much to you and you muttered something about her being bored all day in the caravan. Then you smiled and said that anyway it was much better for Peter to have this big garden to play in. I thought that a little cool of you, but I didn't say so. Perhaps something in my expression made you add that you wouldn't let him worry me.

He doesn't worry me, although it sometimes

gives me a pang to see him running about the place so happily. You don't know that I once had a little son. He was only one year old when he died. I never told you about him and I never will, the last thing I want is for you to be sorry for me. Dilys called her own son David after him. She thought it would please me. Only someone as insensitive as Dilys could have done such a thing. Never mind—that is all long ago and it is the present that matters.

Peter is a good child and no trouble. You try, I know, to keep him near you and as quiet as possible, but of course you can't and I see and hear him all over the garden. He is one of those lucky children who apparently don't need toys, and he plays happily by himself for hours with leaves and sticks and stones. He is a pretty little boy with his mother's dark hair and your blue eyes. I am glad he hasn't got his mother's eyes. You take him home at tea time and wait with him until your wife gets back. If I resent Peter at all, it is because you and I no longer have our afternoon tea together. I miss this very much. He comes up to the house with you in the morning for coffee and I often hear him chattering away to Mrs. Barrett, who approves of him. You eat your midday meal together in the greenhouse, and you rest together under the trees in the orchard. How you dote on that child! I have to admit I'm jealous of Peter. Isn't that absurd? Jealous of a little boy!

In Her Garden

Oddly enough, I am not jealous of your wife, although I wonder if you still sleep with her sometimes. You are both young and you live in such close proximity. I think of your head on the pillow, and hers . . . This thought distresses me, I must admit, but I am not jealous. Mrs. Barrett says that although it's common knowledge that there's no love lost between you, your wife is the jealous one. She says that if you so much as look at another woman there is a fearful scene. "Just like her aunt," Mrs. Barrett said. "Poor old Roper—it's quite a joke in the village."

Mrs. Barrett goes on holiday next week. I shall be the one to give you and Peter your coffee then. I thought you might like a holiday yourself. When I asked you, you shook your head and said, "Where should I go? I like it best here." I was happy that you said it. I don't want to part with you even for a week, but something made me suggest that your wife might think differently. You said that she was free to go where she liked, that she earned her own money. You added, "She won't go, not without me," and then you firmly changed the subject.

I don't want to think about your wife yet I find I often do. Why? When you mention her it is in a tone of complete indifference. I can't be indifferent. There is something horribly potent about her. I won't think of her. I won't let her spoil this golden summer.

In Her Garden

There are only a few more weeks of Peter's holidays. Then I will have you to myself again.

Dearest Ben,

I lay awake most of the night trying to make up my mind. It is a big step to take and would eventually change your life, for the better, I hope. Towards dawn I made my decision and at once fell deeply and dreamlessly asleep.

I have no intention of dying before I must, so I trust that "eventually" will be many years away. It will come though and when it does I will be sustained by the knowledge that you will be secure and that you will have what you have never had before, ease and comfort. Peace and happiness I can't leave you, my beloved Ben. I wish I could.

I was determined to act that very day, so I rang up Mr. Ransom directly after breakfast and asked to see him that morning. I said it was important and at last he said he could fit me in at half-past ten, if I could get there by then.

You were in the yard and you got the Mini out for me. When I told you I was going into town, you asked if you could come too; the big mower had broken down and you needed a spare part. I was rather dismayed, why I don't know. Even if you did know that I was going to see my lawyer, what I intended to do would be a secret between Mr. Ransom and me. I said, "What about Peter?" You assured me that he would en-

joy the drive and you fetched him from the
kitchen where he was talking away to Mrs. Barrett. You assumed that you would drive and I
was only too glad. I like being driven by you.
The Mini is so small that in it we are almost
touching.

You dropped me off in front of Mr. Ransom's
office and we arranged to meet in the car park in
an hour. I thought it would be plenty of time
and that I might even do some necessary shopping. I don't know what happened to the rest of
Mr. Ransom's clients that morning because he
went on with me for what seemed hours, rea-
soned and pleaded. He kept on saying that as an
old friend of my husband he must do all he
could to prevent me from making such a will.
"Not only the house and garden," he said, "but
the money as well to your gardener, a young
man you have known only a few months." He
begged me to think again. Then he told me that
my stepdaughter would be bound to dispute
such a will and when I told him I was sure that
Dilys would respect my wishes and that she was
very well off as it was, he said, "I shouldn't
count on it. No one, when it comes to it, has
enough money." He asked me to think of the
scandal. He said that he was sure I regarded you
as a son but that other people might think differently. I laughed and said, "What, at my age!
That's absurd." I doubt though if Mr. Ransom
was fooled. What does it matter? I stuck to my

guns and he had no choice but to do as I wanted. There are other lawyers and he saw that I was determined.

When at last it was over and I was out of that room, I was exhausted. I could hardly get myself to the car park. You were waiting in the front seat and Peter was asleep in the back. After one look at my face, you opened the door for me and helped me in without a word.

It only remains for me to sign the fair copy of the will and have it witnessed. This I will do in Mr. Ransom's office. I would not want Mrs. Barrett, or anyone else nearer at home, to have an inkling that I have changed my will. Then I shall have done what I can for you.

You needn't have scruples about accepting, Ben. My former bequests to the children and Mrs. Barrett still stand. As for Dilys, she is already quite a wealthy woman and she doesn't want the house. I asked her the other day if she would ever live in it and she said, "Good God, no. Setons is far too big."

On thinking it over, I ask myself if I should tell you, at least give you a hint that would set your mind at rest about the future. You worry over Peter, I know. I haven't made up my mind about this.

I won't write another letter to you. I feel I won't need to, not for some time anyway.

CHAPTER

8

Outside the green oasis of the garden, the September fields were a golden brown; the sun was fierce and there had been little rain for weeks. Grace sat on her camp-stool at the far end of the lawn facing the house. She was finishing a painting that she had begun in June.

Ever since her interview with Mr. Ransom, she had been at peace with herself. No one else would be able to do more for Ben and this knowledge calmed and comforted her and gave her a new strength. She no longer dreamt her disturbing dreams, which were often half-awake fantasies. Perhaps her feeling for Ben was changing. Perhaps this wild and foolish love is turning into something wiser and more suitable, sighed Grace.

She sat back and studied the little painting on her easel. It would amuse Hugh and she looked forward to showing it to him. Behind the spray of lightly sketched in wild roses, an improbably green lawn sloped up to a far-away pink house, her own house in miniature, set slightly askew against a pale blue sky. Nearer, but still in the distance, Ben sat on his big lawn-mower, his fair hair blown back by the speed of his mowing. Every shining detail of the little pictured figure and its machine had been painted with meticulous care. She smiled as she looked at it.

She did not need to turn her head to know that Ben was standing close behind her; she could feel the warmth of his presence. He had made no sound as he approached and she wondered how long he had been there.

"Well, Ben, do you like it?" she asked, and he chuckled.

"Yes, I like it," he said. "That's me on the mower all right. The little house looks as if it might fall down. Why have you made it leaning like that? And the roses aren't real roses, are they? But it's fine, you're clever."

"I'm not clever, far from it."

"Oh yes, you are. There's the things you say and the way you say them, and the things you know. To begin with you know as much about gardening as I do. Then there's not only your painting, you can play the piano. I've heard you sometimes in the evenings."

"I play very badly, just to amuse myself."

"It sounds all right to me."

Grace turned to look at him. He was staring at the painting as if it fascinated him, and she said, "Come and sit down on the grass beside me where I can see you. I can't talk to anyone behind my back."

He hesitated, and she said, "What's the matter?"

"I don't like to—not in front of you."

"Nonsense, sit down."

As he sat where she pointed, he said, "I didn't mean to interrupt you."

"You're not, I've finished."

"I came to tell you there's a tree in the spinney what ought to come down. It's not safe. I'll have to get a man to help me."

"Very well, I'll leave it to you."

He was wearing one of his faded blue shirts, hanging loose from his big shoulders. The pale hair was bleached still paler by the sun. Was it beginning to grow a little thin? It gave her a pang to think that he too would one day grow old. He was thirty, she knew, but to her he had always seemed the personification of youth.

She said, "How is Peter? The place seems very quiet without him."

"He's all right. He brought home a picture he had painted at school. Very proud of it he is. Said to show it to you."

"I would like to see it. Children often paint so very well."

"I didn't. I was hopeless. The teacher used to laugh at me. Before my voice broke I could sing though. My mother wanted me to have lessons and I was so set on it that when my father said it would be a waste of time and money I hid myself and cried, big boy as I was."

In Her Garden

Ben looked up at her and said, "I've never told anyone that before."

This confidence was the fruit of their tea-time talks together. Grace felt flattered and pleased. Before she could say anything, Ben said, "My father was right in a way. I can't sing now, only whistle," and he laughed.

"You can certainly do that," Grace said. "Tell me something about your mother, Ben. Were you fond of her?"

"I suppose so. I can't remember much about her. I wish she could have been like you, it would have made all the difference. There's no one like you."

Grace was silent. This avowal was far from what she needed from him, but it meant a great deal to her. Why had he said it, and did he really mean it? She looked at him searchingly. The blue eyes had their candid, open look. She doubted if he could dissemble if he tried, and why should he want to?

She smiled at him and said as lightly as she could, "Thank you, Ben. That's a great compliment."

He did not smile back. He said, "It's not a compliment, it's the truth. I think the world of you."

If only she could have appeared pleased and touched, nothing more, all would have been well. Grace's control broke. Tears were in her eyes as she stretched her hand out and gently touched his hair. Even then he might have thought this a motherly gesture, but she drew her fingers down his cheek to his mouth in an unmistakable caress.

86

In Her Garden

He drew his head back sharply and she saw that he had reddened with embarrassment. He stared at her with consternation and alarm. She looked away but not before she had seen the alarm change to pity.

Grace's one idea now was to get away. She struggled to stand up and found that she could not move.

Ben was standing over her. He bent down and, putting his arm round her shoulders, helped her to her feet. Grace turned to him and put her head down on his breast. She said brokenly, "Ben—oh, Ben!"

He patted her shoulder and said in a rather loud and matter-of-face voice, "There now, there now, no call to take on so. You're stiff and tired from sitting too long. You've been overdoing it. It's still too hot for you."

She tried to move away from him but he kept his arm round her until she whispered, "I'm all right now. Thank you, Ben. I can manage."

He stood back then and, although she did not look at him, she knew that he was watching her. He said, "I'll see you into the house, and fetch your painting things later. I'll tell Mrs. Barrett that you came over faint and get her to make you a nice cup of tea."

Grace began to laugh, she could not help it, and he said, in a very different voice, "Stop that at once. That won't help. It's not like you," and, putting his hand under her arm, walked her to the house.

Mrs. Barrett, after one look at her, made her lie down on her bed, drew the curtains, and put a cup of strong tea beside her. Grace did not have the energy to protest but managed to object strongly when Mrs. Barrett wanted to telephone for the doctor.

When she was alone the thought came to her that Ben might decide that it would be wiser not to come back. In spite of what had happened, never to see him again was more than she could bear. She could not face him again today, and tomorrow was Wednesday. She would have to wait until Thursday to know. It seemed a long time.

That evening Grace wrote one more letter to Ben, and put it away with the others.

Dearest Ben,

I shall never forgive myself for losing control as I did this morning and for showing only too plainly what I felt. You have been happy in this garden and I suppose that you have a lot to lose, but you may decide not to come back. Even if you come to work on Thursday as usual and try to pretend that it never happened, nothing will be the same again. You will be wary of me, keep your distance. I have spoilt everything, I have lost you, poor fool that I am.

The garden, that Wednesday, was unnaturally quiet and still, or so it seemed to Grace. The sun shone from a clear sky as it had done for weeks. There was not a breath of wind, not a leaf stirred, and the birds were silent. It was as if everything in the garden was in a trance of suspense, as she was.

To avoid Mrs. Barrett, who was inclined to fuss over her, Grace spent the morning well away from the house. At first she tried to occupy herself by taking pelargonium cuttings in the greenhouses, something she usually enjoyed doing. Today she found the greenhouses unbearable, and not only because they were too hot. They reminded her of Ben; everywhere she looked she saw him. This was true of the whole kitchen garden, which was his special domain.

She was less unhappy in the side garden where, determined to keep busy, she spent the time until luncheon tidying the long herbaceous border, clipping, weeding, tying up the tall clumps of Michaelmas daisies. The pink walls of the house soared above her into the blue sky, and she thought of that May morning when she had seen the first swallows, the day Ben had arrived. Was it less than five months ago? The swallows were still there. Soon they would be gathering, and before long they would be gone.

It would have been wiser to spend the long afternoon in the house and to have avoided the garden, but restlessness drove her out to wander up and down the paths, across the lawns and in and out of the orchard. It was hot for late September. The sun glared down and there were few shadows.

That morning, Grace had felt very much alone. The whole place had seemed already deserted, as it would be if Ben did not come back. Now, in midafternoon, as she walked under the orchard trees, suddenly she knew the garden was not empty. Someone was there. She looked round uneasily, searching the spaces between the tree trunks. There was nothing to be seen, no one was following her, and yet she was convinced that she was being watched. Even if that someone was hiding in the garden it was probably some child playing truant from school, curious, mischievous, but meaning no harm. There was no reason to be afraid.

When she came through the gap in the yew hedge into the sunlight of the rose garden, she paused. The roses in the big centre bed were still a blaze of colour and scented the heavy air; the silence was broken by the humming of the bees in the roses, an everyday, peaceful sound. In the background, the flight of stone steps, with their flanking urns, led up to the lawns and the way back to the house.

Anyone following her could not cross this open paved space without being seen. She waited, scanning the dark enclosing wall of yew, anxious now to face her pursuer, if she really were being pursued. She called, "Is anyone there?" Her voice sounded unnecessarily loud in the stillness. There was no response and, after waiting a little longer, she turned towards the steps.

CHAPTER

10

Ben's van was in the yard as usual when Mrs. Barrett arrived on Thursday morning.

She was a little early and expected to find Grace at breakfast in the morning-room. The room was empty, the windows open, the table bare. That's odd, she thought, and she wondered if her Mrs. M. had gone out early and then had forgotten all about breakfast, or if she had overslept. Mrs. Barrett went upstairs and, after knocking, looked into the bedroom. The bed was already made, or perhaps it had not been slept in. What a silly I am, she told herself. If Mrs. M. had overslept the back-door would have been locked.

When she was back in the kitchen, Mrs. Barrett hesitated. The sensible thing to do would be to get on with her work and let Mrs. M. come in from the garden in her own time. The house seemed unnaturally quiet. She was beginning to feel uneasy, why she did not know. After a moment, she went out to look for Ben.

In Her Garden

Ben was where she had thought he would be, in the kitchen garden. He assured her that he had not seen Mrs. Maitland that morning. "It's early yet," he said.

"She's nowhere in the house and the Mini is in the garage, so she must be somewhere in the garden."

"Then why not leave her be? It's a fine day, and her time's her own."

"I'm going to look for her," Mrs. Barrett said. "She hasn't had any breakfast and I won't be easy until I know she's all right. Come with me, Ben."

He seemed reluctant, but he put his hoe down and together they went across the lawn in front of the house. There was no one on the terrace or in the side garden.

"Perhaps she's picking roses before the sun gets too hot," Mrs. Barrett suggested, and they crossed the lawn again, their feet leaving dark imprints in the dew-wet grass.

Mrs. Barrett reached the top of the flight of steps first, she was hurrying now. She paused to look across the rose garden to the empty fields beyond. Then she looked down. Her scream brought Ben to her side and sent a blackbird whirling up and into the yew hedge, calling its alarm note.

Grace lay on her back at the bottom of the steps, her arms flung out. The grey blue of her clothes was much the same colour as the stone beneath her. Her head was twisted at an unnatural angle and they could not see her face.

They knelt beside her and Mrs. Barrett said,

through her tears, "It's a stroke, it must be. We must get her into the house and ring the doctor."

Ben touched one of the outflung hands and bent to lay his head for moment on Grace's breast. "She's not breathing," he said as he straightened himself. He put the silver hair back and looked at her face. The grey eyes stared up at him. He said, "It's no use. She's dead."

Mrs. Barrett cried, "Dead? She can't be. Get the doctor. Carry her into the house, Ben. We can't let her lie there."

"Better not move her until the doctor gets here. It won't make any difference to her. Reckon she's lain there all night. Her clothes are soaking—the dew."

He looked up at the steps. "She must have fallen from the top, poor lady."

"She wasn't one for falling."

"Anyone could trip coming down. Those steps are steep. Should be a rail, I told her so once."

Mrs. Barrett said, "She can't have been coming down. She fell on her back."

Ben stood up and taking his handkerchief from his pocket spread it over Grace's face. "I'll go up to the house now and ring the doctor," he said. "Doctor will know what's best to do. You stay here with her."

Mrs. Barrett clutched his arm. "No, no—I couldn't. You stay, please, Ben. Let me go for Doctor."

"Go on then, and hurry, woman, or you'll miss

him at surgery. I'll stay. I'd do more than that for her."

At the top of the steps Mrs. Barrett looked back. Ben was sitting with his elbows on his knees and his head in his hands.

It was October, a grey day, when Dilys drove up to
the house. She had not been back since the funeral,
that disastrous day when Mr. Ransom had read the
will. The trees along the drive were turning, a few
leaves floated down. Dilys was glad that it was a
cold, dull day; sunlight, the warm, brilliant weather
that had persisted for so long, would have seemed
wrong.

She parked the car in its usual place, picked up her
briefcase, and, taking a key from her bag, opened the
front door. The chill in the hall made her gasp. The
complete silence was unnerving; the house might
have been shut up and deserted for years instead of
weeks.

Dilys closed the door behind her and hesitated,
looking up the staircase as if she expected to see a familiar figure emerge from the shadows. Mrs. Barrett
had left the long curtains drawn across the landing
window and the hall was darker than usual. Dilys was

a woman of little imagination, yet it took all her resolution to make herself cross the open space of the
hall to the morning-room. The sound her heels made
on the polished boards was almost indecently loud.
Suddenly she stood still and looked round. Someone
was standing in the kitchen doorway, watching her.

"Mrs. Barrett! What a shock you gave me." Her
voice shook with relief. "I didn't expect to find you
here."

Mrs. Barrett came towards her. She was wearing
her coat and scarf and carrying a kitchen knife. "And
you gave me a turn, I must say, Mrs. Fenton," she
said. "I'm that jumpy these days. How did you get
in? Mr. Ransom gave me a key, but I thought he
took all the others."

"I still have a key of my own. What are you doing
with that knife, Mrs. Barrett?"

Mrs. Barrett looked a little sheepish. She said, "I
snatched it up when I heard someone in the hall,"
and she added darkly, "You never know these days."

"Have you been coming here regularly?"

"Most mornings, just to air the place and keep it
tidy like. I don't much fancy being alone in the
house, but Mrs. Maitland wouldn't have wanted it to
be neglected. I might even have come now and then
for nothing, but the estate pays me, so Mr. Ransom
says."

Watching Dilys's face, she said, "Ben is in the garden—don't you worry, you needn't set eyes on him.
He never comes near the house, won't set foot in it.

In Her Garden

He works in the garden just as he used to do, and Mr. Ransom pays him too. Seems funny, doesn't it, when I suppose it's his garden."

Dilys said, "It's not his garden yet," and opened the morning-room door.

Mrs. Barrett followed her. "Will you be staying long?"

"Most of the day, I expect." Dilys put the brief-case down on the writing-table by the window. "I'm going through my mother's papers first. I will be down again on Wednesday, the day after tomorrow, to see to her clothes. I want to get it over. Perhaps you would give me a hand with them then?"

"Glad to, though that will be a sad business. Got to be done though, and best done by those who loved her. I'll put the electric heater on for you, it's cold in here. I would have turned the central heating on if I'd known you were coming. What about your lunch?"

"I've brought something with me. Don't let me keep you, Mrs. Barrett. I see that you are ready to be off."

"Yes, I only stay until eleven. I'll leave you to it then. Be sure to lock up carefully, won't you?"

"Of course."

Mrs. Barrett came a step nearer. She said, "It's easy to forget something. I left the pantry window unfastened one day, and someone got into the house."

"How do you know?"

"Nothing had been taken, as far as I could see, but it's difficult to tell in a big house like this. Things had been moved, and the door of her room was wide open when I'm always careful to shut it, and then there was a drawer pulled out."

"It must have been Ben."

"I'm sure it wasn't."

"Did you tell Mr. Ransom?"

"Yes. He said for me to be more careful in future and that he'd inform the police. They are keeping an eye on the place."

"I know. What could this mysterious person have been after?"

"Just snooping, having a look round, if you ask me. Still, it isn't nice."

Dilys said, "I don't suppose it will happen again, Mrs. Barrett. I hope you won't let it put you off from coming here."

"Not me, not after the way Mrs. Maitland remembered me. Not only the money, but her lovely fur jacket. Well, goodbye, Mrs. Fenton. Be seeing you soon."

When Dilys was alone, she took off her coat and sat down at the writing-table. The garden was shrouded in mist, but at the far end of the vista of lawn she could just make out the stone urns that guarded the descent to the rose garden. She winced, and looked quickly away.

It did not take her long to go through the writing-table drawers: a cheque-book, an address book, writing paper, the usual odds and ends. Grace had kept her important papers in the bottom drawer of the bureau that stood against the further wall. This must be tackled next.

In Her Garden

Dilys found that she was reluctant to begin. She wandered round the room, touching the furniture, running her hand along a row of books. Nothing had changed. The room brought Grace vividly before her. Dilys stopped in front of the fireplace and looked up at the portrait she knew so well. This was Grace as she had first seen her when Hubert had brought his new wife home. The painter had caught that ethereal quality that had fascinated the seven-year-old child. The grey, painted eyes looked down at her now with their dreamy, yet quizzical look. "How could you?" Dilys whispered. "Why did you do it? Why?" She blinked tears back, and turned to the bureau.

There were files and long envelopes inscribed with their contents, to her relief all neatly arranged, but the first thing she noticed when she opened the drawer was a rosewood box that she recognized. It was locked.

Somewhere in the writing-table there had been a small key; she had wondered why it had been hidden in one of the drawers. Dilys carried the box to the table and unlocked it. There was nothing inside except several sheets of Grace's blue writing-paper all covered with the familiar bold slanting writing that she had always thought so unlike Grace. Dilys unfolded the top letter, for these she realized were letters, unaddressed and never sent, read the first lines,

My dearest Ben,
I have decided to write to you whenever I feel I must, when I can bear it alone no longer . . .

and dropped it as if it had stung her.

She hesitated, looking out at the garden, but not for long, before she picked up the letter again:

> To me it doesn't make a jot of difference that I'm old enough to be your mother—no, your grandmother! I do not feel towards you as I would towards a son, far from it. I am a woman of no particular age, most painfully and uselessly in love.

As she read this, Dilys said aloud, "No, oh no! Oh, Grace." She turned away, paused irresolutely, and sat down at the writing-table. Her pale face was grim and her hands were shaking as she spread the letters out. All were dated. She put them in order and started to read. When she had finished, Dilys pushed the letters away from her and began to weep, noisily and without restraint, as she had not wept since Grace had died. She did not hear the door open.

Hugh saw her crouching over the table, her dark head down on her folded arms; her shoulders were shaking.

His first thought was to go away as quietly as he could. He had known Dilys a long time. Before they both married he had known her well, but she would probably resent his seeing her in such a state. There was something, though, about this violent grief that worried him. Why now, he wondered? She had been stoical all through the funeral, as he had expected her to be.

In Her Garden

He said, "Dilys, my dear—can I do anything? I'm so sorry," and, having shut the door behind him, went to her.

She sat up and turned a ravaged face to him. He saw that she was making an effort to control herself, and he put his hand on her shoulder as he would have done to any woman who had gone to him for help, as so many did. "Come and sit by the fire," he said. "The worst is over now, isn't it? You'll feel better soon."

Dilys gulped, found her handkerchief, and blew her nose. He saw that the table was strewn with open letters; he recognized Grace's writing. Dilys must have sensed that he was looking at the letters, for she swept them together, and put her hands out, to hide them.

"Is anything the matter?" he asked.

She stood up and walked unsteadily to a chair. "I've had a shock," she managed to say, and the tears began again.

Hugh went to the corner cupboard where Grace had kept her drink. The bottles and glasses were still there. He poured brandy into a glass and gave it to Dilys. "Drink that up," he said briskly, "and then, if you want to, tell me all about it."

"I couldn't. It's too shameful."

"It's those letters, I suppose. From Grace?"

Dilys nodded.

"Letters to you?"

"No! Not to me—far from it."

In Her Garden

He waited, but all she said was, "Desmond didn't want me to come here today. I wish I had listened to him. He's still annoyed with me, you know, disappointed, he says. He thinks that I behaved badly that day, over the will."

"So you did!"

Hugh said it lightly, but he meant it. Dilys had surprised him that day. At one time he had been mildly fond of her. That had not lasted and, as she grew older, he had come to the conclusion that he did not like her. Lately he had resented the way she had nagged Grace about leaving the house. He had thought her, though, a calm, well-bred woman, a good wife, like his own Mavis, and like her in many other ways. He always knew what Mavis was thinking and what she would do. There were no surprises, which could be boring but was peaceful, so different from Grace, who had always been unpredictable and stimulating.

He sighed and, looking at Dilys, remembered the way she had jumped up and, breaking the stunned silence that had followed Mr. Ransom's voice, had cried, "No! It's not possible! She must have been out of her mind. Everything to him, the gardener—someone she had known only a few months."

Mr. Ransom had read the will sitting at Grace's writing-table, here in the morning-room. The two Fentons had sat on the sofa while Hugh and Mavis had been in armchairs near the fire. "I could have written to each of you," Mr. Ransom had begun, "but considering how long a connection I have had with the family and what I have to tell you, I thought it better to ask all concerned to meet me here. I made an exception of Mrs. Barrett, who has a small legacy. It seemed to me that you would want to keep what I have to say to yourselves for as long as possible."

Dilys had interrupted him. "Then why is Ben here?" she had asked.

They had all looked at Ben, who had chosen an upright chair near the door. He glanced at Dilys with obvious dislike, then stared down at the floor.

"You will discover that in a moment, Mrs. Fenton, if you will let me proceed," Mr. Ransom had said. Poor man, Hugh had thought, he isn't exactly enjoying this. I see trouble ahead.

He had been right. Dilys had made a scene. She had accused Ben of doing everything he could to influence Grace, of worming his way into her favour. "Not only the money," she had cried, "the house too, my father's house, everything."

Mr. Ransom had said, when he could make himself heard, "Mrs. Maitland assured me that you did not want the house. You understand, don't you, Mrs. Fenton, that she has left you all her personal possessions, with the exception of her books and one of her paintings, which go to Dr. Grainger, and a diamond brooch to Mrs. Grainger. She has also left you what you want of her furniture."

"Then I'll take all the furniture, every stick of it,"

Dilys cried. "Ben Halden will have an empty house, a shell, if he has it at all."

Ben had spoken for the first time. He got to his feet and confronted them. His usually ruddy face was pale and his blue eyes had darkened. "It will be empty all right without her," he had said. "I don't want the house. I don't want any of it."

Hugh remembered that Desmond had taken Dilys by the arm and had forced her to sit down and that he, himself, and Mr. Ransom had spoken together. "I shouldn't be too hasty, if I were you, Mr. Halden," Mr. Ransom had said, while Hugh had cried, "Wait, Ben—you should think of Peter."

"Why did you take Ben's side that day?" Dilys now asked him.

"You overdid it. You were too fierce, and I like Ben."

"How can you? He's a common schemer—turning a silly old woman's head."

"Dilys! To speak of Grace like that! Your mother was a charming and remarkable woman, most intelligent in her own way."

"She was not my mother, and for the first time in my life, I'm glad of it. I called her a silly old woman. That was being charitable."

Dilys stood up and went to the writing-table. She collected the letters and held them out to him. "Read these," she said, "and you'll see what I mean."

Hugh made no attempt to take them. Still lying back in the armchair with his long legs stretched out,

he looked up and said, "What are they and who were
they written to, if not to you?"

"They are love letters. Love letters to—this . . .
this Ben."

Her voice was hard, scornful. He greatly disliked
her at that moment, but all he said was, "Then why
are they here?"

"She never sent them. Go on, read them."

"I shouldn't dream of reading them. How could
you, Dilys. You astonish me."

"There was no note saying the usual 'In the event
of my death burn these unread,' so of course I read
them. And you must read them too, Hugh. It's not
fair to me if you don't."

"What do you mean?"

"You're judging me without really knowing. You
must understand. I have loved Grace ever since I was
a child. I adored her and thought her a wonderful
person. I have always known that I was not important
to her, but it made no difference. I would have done
anything for her."

Except leave her alone, Hugh thought, but he did
not say it. He said, "Well then?"

"Don't you see, she has let me down. It's—it's a
betrayal. Read them and you'll understand."

"Dilys, you're behaving like an angry, disillu-
sioned schoolgirl," Hugh said with irritation. " 'Let
me down'—what a thing to say." But he sat up and
took the letters. While he read them, Dilys stood at
the window with her back to him, looking out at the
garden.

In Her Garden

When he had finished, he said, "Poor, poor, dear Grace."

Dilys threw herself down in the chair opposite him and hid her face in her hands. She said in a muffled voice, "You see?"

"I can't imagine why I didn't see it before," Hugh said slowly. "It's obvious now."

"I realized she was getting a thing about him," Dilys said, "but I thought she was beginning to think of him as a son, that was bad enough. Her own son died as a baby, you know."

"Yes, I know."

"I always hoped my David would take his place."

Hugh could find nothing to say to that, and Dilys went on, "I never dreamt of this. Love, that kind of love, at her age. It's shocking."

"Is it? Why? Physical love is not the monopoly of the young or even the middle-aged. There's nothing shocking in those letters. Nothing to make such a fuss about."

"How can you say that?"

"I do."

"Other people will think differently."

"Other people? Dilys—surely you are going to burn those letters here and now?"

"I'm not. I'll show them to Desmond."

"If I know Desmond, he'll refuse to read them. He was fond of Grace."

"He'll read them all right."

With a sudden movement that took him by surprise, Dilys sprang up and snatched the letters from him. He made as if to get up, then sat back again.

"Think again, Dilys, please," he said. "Let me burn them now. I have my lighter."

"Certainly not. I have a use for those letters."

"What possible use could you have?"

Dilys put the letters into her briefcase and turned back to face him. "Desmond thinks I should bow to Grace's wishes," she said. "I promised him not to do anything in a hurry, but if I decide to contest that will, those letters could be important. They could show undue influence, or that Grace was not in her right mind."

"She was very much in her right mind. I shall say so, in court if necessary."

Dilys glared at him and he said, "Think of the scandal, of the publicity. I've a good mind to make you give me those letters." He got up. "Give them to me, Dilys."

"I won't. If you touch me, I'll ring up the police. I'll have you up for assault. Now that would be a scandal!"

"Don't be an ass!"

"I mean it, and now that I come to think of it, what are you doing here? How did you get in?"

"I thought that Mrs. Barrett might still be here, but I found the front door open so I walked in. I came to choose my picture, Mr. Ransom said I could. The one I particularly wanted isn't upstairs in the studio so I thought it must still be behind the sofa. I last saw it there."

In Her Garden

As he went to the sofa, Dilys turned away and began to walk up and down the room. She was frowning and she did not hear him say, "There are two canvases here, my narcissi and another. I wonder when she painted it." He set the canvas up on the sofa and stepped back to look at it.

Dilys paused beside him as he gave an exclamation of delight. "Come and look at this," he said. "Grace certainly had something."

Dilys was silent, and he said, "That's Ben on the mower, of course."

"I never knew she could paint like that," Dilys said slowly. "For a moment I could almost—no! It's absurd—Grace and that lout! But that's how she saw him, I suppose."

"Yes, larger than life, a radiant, youthful, golden Ben. As I said—poor Grace. What shall I do with it, Dilys? Shall I put it back where it came from?"

"No, leave it here on the sofa. I'll take it home this evening. Perhaps I'll show it to Desmond, then I'll decide what to do with it."

Hugh looked at her searchingly. "What's in your mind, Dilys?" he asked. "You're not thinking of destroying that lovely little painting? That would be wicked."

Dilys did not answer and he said, "Give it to me."

"Certainly not." She turned her back on the canvas and went once more to the window. Hugh said, watching her, "You can't forgive Grace, can you? You are getting at her through Ben."

In Her Garden

"That's nonsense. I've disliked and distrusted him from the first moment I saw him."

If there is such a thing as love at first sight, why should there not be its opposite, Hugh asked himself. Aloud he said, "Dislike—you hate him."

"That would be natural, surely?"

"None of this is his fault. Grace makes that clear in those letters."

"Does she? Not to me."

"Doesn't it occur to you to be glad that he made her so happy all her last summer?"

"I don't think she was happy. She was in a very nervous state, thin and strained."

Hugh sighed and gave it up. "Well, I'll take my picture and go now," he said. "I'm doing no good here. Goodbye, Dilys."

She said, "Wait—I've been thinking."

Hugh paused at the door and looked back at her.

"Dr. Sands wasn't altogether satisfied that Grace's death was an accident, was he?" she asked.

He put the picture down and came back into the room. "What's in your head now, Dilys?" he said. "Why bring that up now after all this time?"

"You haven't answered my question."

"I suppose not, not altogether."

"Why wasn't he satisfied?"

"There were one or two small points, all of which could be explained. He is an overconscientious, earnest fellow. If only I had been in surgery that morning!"

"So you yourself are sure she fell, that she wasn't pushed?"

"Dilys! What a thing to say! You heard the verdict at the inquest, 'Death by misadventure.' "

"I heard the medical evidence too. And it's not usual to fall when going up steps, is it?"

He stared at her in dismay, and said, "You are seriously suggesting that someone . . ." He could not go on.

She nodded, and he said, after a moment, "Who?"

"Ben, of course."

"Now listen, Dilys." Hugh was furious. "You had better be careful. You are letting your feeling against Ben run away with you. Grace died on a Wednesday, sometime between midday and early evening, they think. Ben was working in my garden all that day."

"Are you sure? Did you see him every minute of that time, you or Mavis?"

"Not every minute, of course, but most of the time. Can you really think that Ben—what wicked nonsense! Why should he, for one thing?"

"It's a great deal of money to him. He was badly off."

"But he had no idea that Grace had left him anything. It was as much a shock to him as to everyone else."

"So he says. He could have known. Remember Grace's letter? The one written after she had seen Mr. Ransom? She wrote that she was thinking of telling him what she had done."

"I doubt if she did."

"We'll never know, I suppose, if he sticks to his story."

There was silence as they faced one another. Then Dilys said, "Let that go, for the moment. Suppose that it was not deliberate. Suppose that something brought Ben back, on his way home perhaps, and Grace saw him. We know from her last letter of the scene between them when, as she says, she lost control and we know how he responded then. There could have been another scene, there at the top of the steps. Perhaps she put her arms round him, begged, and he recoiled. Perhaps he pushed her away and she fell. Not deliberate, you see, but manslaughter all the same."

For a moment Hugh could not speak, or bring himself to look at her. At last he said, "I had no idea that you had such a lurid imagination, Dilys. Even if it could have happened as you say, do you really think that Ben would slink away and leave Grace lying there all night?"

"She was dead. There was nothing to be done, and he must have been afraid."

Hugh controlled himself with difficulty. He said, as quietly as he could, "You horrify me, Dilys. I know that you have had a shock and that you are not yourself today, but I begin to think that you are unbalanced where Ben is concerned. To go to such lengths over this money . . ."

"It's not the money, or even the house. It's the affront."

"An affront? From whom?"

"From Grace, of course. That painting was the last straw."

"I don't understand."

"It is—flagrant. Can't you see that?"

"You mean to depict Ben as she did?"

"Yes, and if you want to know, it has made up my mind for me."

"To do what? To contest the will?"

"That, to begin with. I'll take these letters home and read them carefully. Then I'll probably show them to the police."

Dilys turned her back on him and sat down at the writing-table again.

He said, "I should think very carefully before you do that. Consult Desmond, to begin with. You don't realize what it could mean, not only to Ben, but to all of us. All the village would be agog. The press would get hold of it and Grace's name would be in every cheap rag. Think, Dilys, I beg you."

Dilys said, "I think you had better go now, Hugh. Leave me alone."

Hugh put his picture in the back of his car and got into the driving seat. He switched the ignition on, then turned it off again. There were a couple of visits he ought to make before lunch and he had promised Mavis not to be late; it was more important though to see Ben, and to see him now. With an angry glance up at the house, he slammed the door and went in search of him.

A light drizzle added to the grey depression of the day. Wishing that he had listened to Mavis when she advised him that morning to take a raincoat, he followed the drive round the front of the house. Dead leaves were soggy underfoot, and he thought that the pink walls looked out of place, even foolish in the rain. In Hubert's time it had been a white house and the change Grace had made caused much comment in the village. Ben's van was in the yard, parked in front of the Mini. Whose Mini was it now? "All my personal possessions," the will had said. The sooner everything was settled the better, but when would that be? Hugh sighed.

He had thought that on this raw, damp day Ben might be found in the greenhouses, but as he went into the kitchen garden, he saw him in the distance, back turned, learning on a pitchfork in front of a slow-burning bonfire. Hugh's footsteps sounded on the path, but Ben must have been deep in thought. He did not turn his head until Hugh said close behind him, "Morning, Ben." Then he swung round, as startled as if he had been woken from a dream.

To Hugh's eyes, Ben did not look well. His skin, perhaps because the summer tan was wearing off, was sallow and he was definitely thinner. He was wearing a shabby brown jacket with too short sleeves.

"Oh, it's you, Doctor," he said. He did not say, "What do you want?"; his tone implied it.

"I thought I'd drop in to see how you are getting on, and I want a word with you."

"I'm all right."

"You don't look it."

Ben flung a forkful of rubbish onto the fire. There was a brief spurt of flame, and blue smoke wound up, eddying and curling, to vanish into the grey sky. He said, "I can't get used to her not being here, somewhere in the garden. There ought to be some sign of her, that's what I feel, but there's nothing, nothing."

"I know. 'My dead have disappeared like burnt smoke.' "

"Who said that?"

"A favourite author of hers. Listen, Ben, have you done anything about a lawyer?"

"No, I haven't."

"You should, as soon as possible. Mr. Ransom would recommend someone. Would you like me to ask him?"

"Why not Mr. Ransom himself? I liked him."

"He will represent Mrs. Fenton. She will probably contest the will, you know."

"So she said that day, and she'll stick to it. That one! I can't stand her, and she's had it in for me from the start."

"You can't expect her to be pleased."

"No, I don't. It's only natural, I suppose, well off as she is, but she's so bloody vindictive, she hates my guts. If it was someone else wanting to upset that will, I might play along, let it go."

In Her Garden

"Mrs. Maitland wanted you to have her house and money. You shouldn't forget that."

"I don't forget it. Poor lady, she meant well, but from now on there'll be nothing but trouble, it won't turn out as she meant. This garden now, it means a lot to me. How can I keep it? Whatever happens, I'll have to clear out. How can I stay with the things they'll say about me? Already they look at me in the pub—I can't go there anymore. No, she shouldn't of done it."

Hugh hesitated and then said, "She was very fond of you, Ben."

Ben looked away. He said, sadly, "I know." He faced Hugh again and cried, "And I was fond of her. I tell you I thought the world of her. There was no one like her and won't be again. I'd have done anything for her, anything."

He turned back to the bonfire, and Hugh was silent. At last Hugh said, "What about your wife? What does she think of all this? How is she taking it?"

Ben stirred the fire violently, sending a flame soaring, before he answered. "She's taking it all right. She's on top of the world now and talking, talking all over the place, about what she's going to do now she has money, making plans, jabbering away, driving me out of my mind. I try to stop her, tell her that it's all in the air and not to count on it. I told her that Mrs. Fenton is bound to do all she can to upset the will. It's no use though. She's seen herself here, lording it in the house; it's gone to her head. And she's all over me now. I'm a success at last. Do you know what she said to me? She said that I'd been very clever. I nearly hit her then."

He stopped abruptly and looked at Hugh. "Funny thing is that she was very down after Mrs. Maitland died. If I hadn't known better I'd have thought that she was sorry for all the things she'd said about the poor lady."

Hugh said, "Perhaps if this business turns out well for you and you have money, you two might separate, get right away from each other. It might be better for Peter in the long run."

"She's his mother, no getting away from that, and she'd never let me go."

He threw the pitchfork down and turned up the collar of his jacket. "I shouldn't be talking like this," he said. "You're getting wet, standing there listening to me saying what I oughtn't; she's my wife after all. Trouble is I've got into the way of talking and I've no one to talk to now. Let's go into the greenhouse if you've anything else to say to me."

As they walked together down the path, Hugh wondered if he ought to warn Ben, give him a hint of what was in Dilys's mind. He decided against it. Desmond might intervene, Dilys might think better of it. Better leave it alone, he said to himself, and to Ben he said, "We must arrange a good lawyer for you. I'll see to it at once. That's what I came to say."

In Her Garden

On this overcast day, it was growing dark before
Dilys had finished with Grace's papers. As she
switched on the table lamp, she remembered Mrs.
Barrett saying, "Be sure to lock up carefully, won't
you?" Mrs. Barrett had said that someone had got
into the house through the pantry window, which
had been left unfastened. Dilys hoped that Mrs. Barrett had locked up efficiently today, but she supposed
that she ought to go round the house to check that all
was well.

She went into the dark empty kitchen and, having
switched on the lights, tried the back-door. It was
safely locked, and so were the scullery and pantry
windows. Surely there was no need to check the rest
of the house. She was tired and distressed and longed
to go home. Dilys went back to the morning-room,
put on her coat, picked up her briefcase, and turned
to the sofa. She had heard nothing, seen no one, yet
the little canvas was gone.

For a moment Dilys could only stare at the place
where it had been, then she looked behind the sofa
and round the room. Grace's painting had vanished as
if it had never been.

Ben, she thought at once, it must be Ben—but
how could Ben have known where the painting was?
Hugh knew. He had put the canvas on the sofa himself. He was afraid that she would destroy it and he
had sneaked in and taken it while she was in the
kitchen. It was odd that she had not heard his car,
but perhaps he had left it down the drive. When she

got home, she would ring up and tell him what she thought of him.

Dilys stood in the hall listening intently, although there was nothing to hear. She told herself there was no reason to feel so uneasy—of course the house was empty. All she had to do was shut the front door behind her and drive thankfully away.

12

On Wednesday afternoon Dilys and Mrs. Barrett were busy in the big room that had been Grace's bedroom. The bed, chaise-longue, and every chair were covered with piles of clothes.

"Considering that she nearly always wore slacks and pullovers, there is much more than I thought there would be," Dilys said. "She can never have thrown anything away."

"Mrs. Maitland could look very smart when she wanted to, and she always said that if you kept clothes long enough, they came into fashion again. She hated shopping, you know."

"Of course I know." Dilys spoke more sharply than perhaps she had meant to. Mrs. Barrett had annoyed her several times that day, intentionally or not it was difficult to tell. Her manner, too, had been odd. Perhaps it had been a mistake to say, about the jumble, that so many people had had a chance to look it over before it got to the sale that only the rubbish was left. Not very tactful because Mrs. Barrett was on the committee, even if it were true. Instead of chattering away, recounting the usual gossip, Mrs. Barrett had been unusually silent. Dilys would have liked to know what the village thought of Ben's inheritance. Why should she care, but she did.

"What about this coat?" Mrs. Barrett said. "It's worn but still good."

"The nuns will find a use for it among their old people. Put it on the second pile."

Mrs. Barrett did as she was told, then looked at Dilys. "Is it true what's being said about Mrs. Maitland's will," she asked, "that you're going to try to change it?"

"How did you hear that?"

"It's all over the village. Sandra told her aunt. Very bitter, Mrs. Roper is. I wouldn't go near the shop if I was you, Mrs. Fenton."

"I have no reason to go near the shop, but if I had, I wouldn't let Mrs. Roper stop me. I'm sure most people agree that I'm in the right."

Mrs. Barrett looked doubtful. She said slowly, "Well, I don't know about that. The younger ones are all for Ben, think it's a bit of a lark, while some others don't think it's right he should have the house. It's a family house, after all. Your grandfather bought it off the Dancys, didn't he?"

"He did. What else do people say?"

"Some think the money is a different matter, you and Mr. Fenton being well off, I mean."

In Her Garden

"I have my children to think of. My poor step-mother must have been out of her mind. She didn't know what she was doing."

Mrs. Barrett turned away. She muttered something that sounded like "She knew all right."

Dilys decided to ignore this. She said briskly, "Well, we've finished at last. The big pile is for Oxfam, the smaller for the nuns, and the rest for the jumble sale. Now we'll pack all we can in these suitcases and make a bundle of the rest. Perhaps you'll help me to load the car. The jumble we'll leave in the hall."

They were standing in the hall taking a last look round when she said, "Have you arranged for someone to call for the jumble?"

"Yes, on Friday morning, round twelve. I said I'd be here."

"Good, you've been very helpful, Mrs. Barrett. I don't know what I would have done without you."

When the car was loaded and Mrs. Barrett had chugged off down the drive, Dilys went back into the house. She had forgotten her bag, which she must have left in the morning-room where she and Mrs. Barrett had paused in their labours for the sherry and sandwiches she had brought with her.

Dilys looked at her watch as she closed the front door behind her. It was nearly half-past three. She was tired and depressed. Sorting Grace's clothes, handling her belongings had been a strain and had distressed her more than she had expected. She leant for a moment against the door, then pulled herself together and went into the morning-room.

Her bag was on the writing-table. It was lucky that she had forgotten it because the electric fire was still on. Mrs. Barrett, too, must have felt the strain. I was right not to tell her that someone had been in the house again on Monday, Dilys thought. If Mrs. Barrett knew that the painting had been snatched away like that, she might decide not to come here again. If Hugh had not taken it, it must have been Ben, but Mrs. Barrett would never believe it. Dilys picked up the bag and turned back to the hall. As she crossed it, somewhere upstairs a door was closed.

She stood still, wondering if she had imagined this small but definite sound, and knowing that she had not. Someone, making no attempt at concealment, was walking along the upstairs corridor. She called out, "Who's there? Come down at once or I'll call the police."

There was no answer, and the footsteps stopped.

Her first instinct was to rush out of the house and drive away to call the police from the village, but she was angry now. Anyone could have slipped into the house while she and Mrs. Barrett were busy. She was sure though that it was Ben up there and she was not afraid of Ben. Mrs. Barrett had said that he never set foot in the house. How could she know what he did when she was not there? He quite likely thought that he had a right to go where he liked and it was possible that Grace, in her foolishness, had given him a key.

This thought enraged Dilys. She started up the

stairs, and stopped. She had forgotten that it was Wednesday, and it was not yet four. She must find out if Ben was still working in Hugh's garden. Dilys hurried back into the morning-room.

The number, infuriatingly, was engaged. Mavis must be having one of her interminable conversations. The only thing to do was to try again in a few minutes. Dilys had left the door open, and as she put the receiver back, she heard someone running down the stairs.

The hall was empty. As she stood there, wondering what to do, from the closed door of the drawing-room the piano sounded loudly. Someone was running a hand over the keys from treble to bass.

This unexpected, discordant jangling had been deliberately made to mock and provoke her. Dilys ran across the hall. Once again she was too late. The keyboard of the piano was open, but there was no one there. The long curtains billowed into the room from the open window. Whoever had been in the house had gone that way.

Dilys looked out at the deserted terrace. There was no sign of a fleeing figure. Anyone could have slipped round the side of the house to make off down the drive. She locked the window, closed the keyboard, and went back to the morning-room.

This time Mavis answered. "Ben?" she said. "No, he's not here at the moment. Hugh sent him to fetch some plants from the Nurseries; he should be back at any moment. Do you want to speak to him?"

In Her Garden

Dilys's denial was perhaps too vehement because Mavis asked, "Is anything the matter, Dilys? You sound upset. You're up at the house, aren't you? Mrs. Barrett told me."

It was a relief to talk to calm, level-headed Mavis. Dilys told her exactly what had happened and Mavis was sympathetic, but cautious. "You don't know that it was Ben," she said. "It might have been anyone. I should certainly let the police know that someone had been in the house, but if you told them you were sure it was Ben, they might say that he had as much right as you to be there." That annoyed Dilys, and she refused a suggestion that she should come round for a rest and a cup of tea. "You sound as if you could do with one," Mavis said. "Hugh will be back soon and you can tell him all about it."

Dilys did not want to meet Hugh. Their last encounter had hardly been pleasant, and when she telephoned on Monday evening he had not been helpful. "No, Dilys, I didn't sneak in, as you put it. I didn't take the painting," he had said. "I might have done if I'd thought of it. I wish I had." Then Ben would probably be back at work when she got there and even the sight of the white van waiting innocently outside the house would seem to mock her, as the piano had done. She thanked Mavis, and rang off.

She did not wait to ring up the police. I'll do it when I get home, she told herself. I simply must get out of this house.

When she was safely in her car she felt better. She

was still shaken, and there was the long drive home to face. All the same, she decided there and then to go and see Mr. Ransom. Desmond would probably be angry. That could not be helped, and once it was done he would have to accept it without more argument.

It was a quarter to four. If she drove fast Mr. Ransom should still be in his office when she reached it. The sensible thing to do would be to go back to the morning-room, ring him up, and ask him to wait for her. Dilys knew that nothing would induce her to go into the darkening house again.

CHAPTER

13

The next day Dilys drove down from London again. She left the flat soon after breakfast, having written a note for Desmond to find when he came back that evening. "I think we would be better apart for a few days until our tempers have cooled. I shall be at the King's Arms if you have to contact me. There is plenty of food in the refrigerator and freezer if you don't want to go to your club."

Never before, in all their married life, had they had such a quarrel. Desmond had been rather put out when she had come back late the evening before and then had to ask him to help her unload the car. She had waited until after dinner when he was in a better mood to tell him she had seen Mr. Ransom. He had been vexed, as she had expected him to be. "Why are you so set on this?" he had asked her. "We don't really need the money and you don't want the house. I don't understand you, Dilys." As Mr. Ransom had done, he warned her that the case might very well go against her. "Think how very unpleasant it will be for everyone," he said, as Hugh had done. "Much better to think of dear Grace and leave it alone. This Ben Halden seems a decent fellow. Why are you so vindictive?"

In answer she had shown him Grace's letters, and had insisted, as she had done to Hugh, that in fairness to her he must read them. Mr. Ransom had been distressed when she had told him about the letters, although he had agreed that they might strengthen her case, but Desmond had demanded to know why she had not destroyed them at once, as anyone who loved Grace would have done. That had made her really angry and she had cried, "It's because I loved Grace. You see, I'm sure that her death was no accident, that she was pushed down the steps; that's why I'm going to show those letters to the police."

Desmond had been horrified and furious and had soon reduced her to tears. "Everyone is against me," she had sobbed. "You, Hugh, everyone, but you can't stop me. I'm going to do it, it's only right."

Now Dilys parked the car in front of the inn, unpacked her suitcase in the bedroom she had chosen because it looked over the garden instead of the village street, and ordered coffee in the little empty lounge. In her present mood, the place was almost painfully familiar. As a girl she had often been here with her father, sometimes with Grace too. She was glad that the inn had changed hands. The new managers would not talk to her of Grace as the Jonsons would have done.

In Her Garden

As she drank her coffee she decided to go at once to the Nurseries to find out what time Ben had been there yesterday. First though, she would ring up Mr. Ransom and Mavis. He might want to see her again, and Mavis would be sure to hear sooner or later that she was in the village and be offended that she had not gone to her and Hugh. There were other friends who would have been glad to have her, but she was feeling sore and sick at heart, and preferred to be alone.

Mr. Ransom had papers for her to sign and made an appointment with her for the following morning. To her surprise, Mavis seemed relieved that she had elected to stay at the King's Arms. "Hugh is very angry with you," Mavis said. "He won't tell me why. He's out all today so do come to luncheon. I'm longing to hear all about it."

The day was still misty, but gleams of pale sunlight heightened the autumn colours in the woods. Dilys had driven through these narrow winding lanes many times with Grace. As she drove, she found that she was thinking of Grace, not with the bitterness of the last weeks, but sadly, and with longing. By the time she reached the Nurseries, her mood had changed. She walked briskly through the range of glasshouses, looking for the foreman she remembered as always being attentive and helpful—Tucker, yes, that was the name.

When she found him, she had to listen to his regrets and condolences. "Twenty years I've known Mrs. Maitland," he lamented. "A fine lady. It won't

seem the same without her." It was with some difficulty that she managed to change the subject to Ben
Halden.

"Yesterday? Plants for Dr. Grainger?" Tucker
asked. "Let's go to the office. The girl there will
know." Luckily this girl remembered Ben and was
able to fix the time he arrived as she had just come
back from her lunch break at half-past two. So Ben
could have been in Setons, Dilys thought, as she
drove away. He must have left the van by the side
gate and sneaked in, as the front door was open. I
wonder if Mavis knows when he got back with those
plants. I must ask her.

For the first time Dilys wondered why Ben should
have gone to the house at all that Wednesday afternoon. He could have known from Mrs. Barrett that
she, Dilys, would be there. Had he wanted to spy on
her, find out what she and Mrs. Barrett were doing?
When she came back to the house unexpectedly, had
he tried to frighten her away? He probably considered
that she had no right to be there.

Dilys was certain now that the unseen presence in
the house had been Ben. It had been clever of her to
think of going to the Nurseries, but she did not feel
pleased with herself. Desmond had called her vindictive, which surely wasn't true. He had lost his temper
and said many unkind things, which she must try to
forget. As she drove slowly towards the village, seeing nothing of the autumnal countryside, she heard
his voice again, warning her that she would cause dis-

tress to innocent people, and asking her if she had thought of Ben's wife and child. She had not given the wife a thought since, long ago, she had told Grace that she was sorry for a girl whose husband worked such long hours. "You needn't be," Grace had said. It must be hard to learn that the riches you expected may not be yours after all. I ought to feel sorry for her now, Dilys thought, although the girl means nothing to me. I have never even seen her.

She had reached the village and was passing the shop where she remembered Grace telling her Ben's wife worked. Dilys stopped the car and got out. If she had given herself time to think, she might have remembered Mrs. Barrett's warning, but she opened the door and went in.

The shop was crowded. As Dilys looked round, silence fell. She felt that every eye was on her and that most of those eyes were hostile.

It was too late to retreat and Dilys went boldly up to the counter, ignoring the queue, and faced a grim-faced Mrs. Roper. Grace had greatly disliked this woman, whom Dilys had always found amiable and obliging. There was nothing amiable about her today.

"Good morning, Mrs. Roper," Dilys said in her assured, slightly condescending manner. "Is Mrs. Halden here?"

Mrs. Roper glared at her. "She is not. I'm surprised at your asking, Mrs. Fenton."

"Can you tell me where I can find her?"

In Her Garden

Mrs. Roper did not answer, but a woman standing next to Dilys said eagerly, "Sandra's Peter is poorly and her husband had to go into town on business, so she's staying at home all day—back at the Site, that is. I live there too."

Mrs. Roper rounded on her. "Who asked you to put your oar in, Betty March?" she said angrily and, turning to Dilys, "You leave my poor niece alone. You've done enough harm as it is."

Her black eyes went insolently from Dilys's dark head with its well-groomed hair, over her expensive clothes to her expensive shoes. She turned her head to look out of the window at Dilys's long, shining car, and smiled unpleasantly. "Some people can never have enough, can they?" she said to the attentive shoppers. "Greedy, that's what some people are." She leaned over the counter and said directly to Dilys, "I'll trouble you to get yourself out of my shop, Mrs. Fenton. You're not welcome here."

Dilys retreated with as much dignity as she could muster, being careful to shut the shop door gently behind her. Her cheeks were burning. She paused by the car to look at her watch before driving away. It was half-past twelve and she would be late for Mavis, but she was determined now to see Ben's wife; she must know what she was like, see how she lived; it was, Dilys now felt, her duty. If the case went against Ben, as she was sure it would, perhaps something could be done for his wife and child. None of this was their fault.

The accusation of greed rankled. It was not greed,

In Her Garden

Dilys told herself, that had resolved her to dispute Grace's will; it was resentment and anger. She drove as fast as she dared through the village to the Site.

The sun had dispelled the mist and shone on the rows of caravans, which all looked much alike to Dilys. She had never been on the Site before and, as many people did, had always averted her head if she found herself driving past it. Leaving her car, as Grace had done many months ago, at the wide gap in the hedge that was the entrance to this caravan park, she walked over the worn grass, looking for someone to direct her. There appeared to be no one about, so she knocked on the door of the first caravan she came to. The inmates were evidently busy with their midday meal; a strong smell of cooking flowed out when the door was opened. A large woman in a flowered overall filled most of the doorway, but Dilys had a glimpse of a laid table and several people sitting round it.

"Halden?" the woman said, as if she had never heard the name. Her eyes examined Dilys, much as Mrs. Roper's had done, and Dilys began to wish she hadn't come. Once again she was met with suspicion and hostility. What could she expect from Ben's wife?

"Yes, Halden," she repeated firmly.

"He's bound to be out."

"It's Mrs. Halden I've come to see. Please tell me which caravan is hers."

A small ginger-haired boy edged round the woman. "I'll show the lady," he said.

"You get back inside and eat your dinner."

In Her Garden

"I've finished." The child grinned at Dilys, who felt cheered. He was a plain little boy with a bad cold, but no one else had smiled at her that day. He pushed past the woman and hurried off, turning his head at a safe distance to see if Dilys were following him.

The Haldens' caravan was not far away. When her guide reached it, he waited for her to catch up with him. "That's it," he said, "and she's in all right. I see'd her this morning. Like me to knock?"

"No thanks, I'll do that." Dilys opened her bag. "Here's something for you to buy sweets with."

He took the money without comment and slipped it into his pocket. "Like me to keep an eye on your car?" he asked, and added, "My gran kept me back from school because I woke up with a tempature and I've got nothing to do."

"Then you shouldn't be out of doors without a coat," Dilys told him. He grinned at her again and ran off.

The door opened before she could climb the step and knock. Ben's wife, who was a far smaller and slighter edition of Mrs. Roper, looked down at her enquiringly. The white face, framed in coal black hair, was striking—never before had Dilys seen such large and such black eyes. It was, though, a bad-tempered, discontented little face.

"Mrs. Halden?" Dilys said.

"Yes, that's me."

As she said it, the girl's expression changed, became almost venomous. She drew back and glared at Dilys.

In Her Garden

"It's Mrs. Fenton, isn't it?" she said in a flat, rather breathless and hoarse young voice. "You get out of here."

Dilys ignored this. "How do you know who I am?" she asked. "You've never seen me before, or I you."

"I've seen you all right."

"Have you? I can't imagine where."

The girl was silent. Dilys was sure that the door was about to be shut in her face, and she said quickly, "Can I come in for a minute?"

"Why should you? Bloody cheek."

"I must—I want to talk to you."

There was a moment's hesitation. Dilys, watching the sullen young face, saw hostility give way to a stirring of interest and—was it hope? The girl stood back and motioned her inside.

The caravan was roomier than she had imagined. The door opened into a sitting-room that at first sight looked comfortable enough. She wondered where the kitchen was; a smell of cooking pervaded the place. Through an open doorway she saw an unmade bed in which a child was sitting upright against the pillows, staring at her with startled blue eyes.

Dilys thought, I would hate to live here, but if I had to it would be a pleasanter place—Ben's wife must be a lazy little slut. The room was untidy, shabby, dirty. A towel-horse held drying wash and toys littered the floor. A portable television set stood in what was obviously the place of honour.

She saw that there had been a rather pathetic attempt at decoration. Prints that looked as if they had been cut from a calendar were tacked to the wall and a shelf held a collection of china ornaments, mugs, vases, a teapot, and several china animals. Among them was what looked like a small Staffordshire dog. Dilys's eye was caught and held.

She glanced at the girl, who was watching her from under long, black eyelashes, and said, "I was admiring your collection. That little dog, there in the middle, is exactly like one I was allowed to play with when I was a child. It belonged to my father and was kept in the cabinet in our drawing-room. Can I have a closer look at it?"

The girl did not move. She said, "Ben gave it to Peter. Found it in the market, he said. It's too good for Peter to break, so I put it up there."

Dilys could not very well push past her to reach the shelf and, after all, such china dogs were not uncommon. She sat down at the table, which was covered with a stained cloth and laid for two. At least it's not oilcloth, she thought.

"How is your little boy?" she asked. "I hear that he hasn't been well."

"Peter's all right. Could have gone to school if you ask me, but his father fusses over him. 'Keep him in bed one more day,' he said. All very well for him, it's me that has to stay stuck here. Putting my aunt out and all."

"I should have thought that your husband could have taken time off from the garden for once," Dilys said.

In Her Garden

"Of course he could. It's his garden, after all." The girl threw a defiant glance at Dilys, and said, "He would have too, he likes looking after Peter, but he had to go into town to see a lawyer. Doctor made an appointment for him."

She turned her head to look at a clock on the shelf behind her and said, "I thought he'd be back by now to see how Peter is and for something to eat. I've taken the trouble to lay his place and get something ready for him. He must have gone straight back to that old garden, in his good clothes and all. Even now *she's* not there, he can't keep away."

Dilys thought it better to ignore this. She could feel the packet of letters in the bag on her lap, and she wondered how much Ben's wife knew, or suspected. She said, "I wish you would sit down. It's difficult to talk to someone standing up. Your name is Sandra, isn't it?"

The girl nodded and sat down opposite Dilys. The child called out from the bedroom and his mother answered, without turning her head, "You be quiet, Pete, the lady wants to talk to me." She looked at Dilys and said, "Well, what have you got to say? There's only one thing I want to hear."

Dilys did not answer, and Sandra said, "Then why have you come?"

Dilys was not at all sure why she had come. It had seemed to her that she ought to see Ben's wife and home, but now that she was here, she did not know what to say or do. She stared across the table at the thin white face and thought, This is an unhappy girl, terribly on edge and overstrained. I must be careful.

As she struggled for words, Peter began to whine and Sandra, exclaiming impatiently, jumped up and seized the little television set.

"He's mad about this," she said, "would watch it all day if I let him." She carried the set into the bedroom, and, when she came back, shut the door firmly. "That will keep him quiet for a bit," she said as she sat down again. "I've turned the sound low."

Dilys smiled, glad to have something easy to say at last. "Television has its uses. Don't you find it a blessing?"

"Perhaps I do, but I wanted to send this set back. It was a present from *her,* of course. We can't afford no television sets. She would have liked to give it to Ben, I'm sure, but she knew that, although he's soft and finds it difficult to say no to anyone except me, he wouldn't have taken it, so she goes and gives it to Peter. Cunning, that's what she was, a bad, sly old bitch."

The bitterness in this sudden spate of words startled Dilys. She said, "Don't—my mother wasn't like that. Don't say such things. You shouldn't speak evil of the dead."

The look in the black eyes was frightening. The hoarse voice cried, "Yes, she's dead, and I'm glad, do you hear? She deserved to die. She was old, old, but she got him, he thought the world of her. I've sat here for hours knowing he was up there with her, and imagining things. You don't know."

In Her Garden

To Dilys's dismay, Sandra put her head down on the table and began to cry, noisily, like a child.

Dilys stretched her hand out involuntarily to touch the tumbled black hair. "Don't—please don't," she pleaded.

The girl lifted her head and sat up. She said, between sobs, "All that money and the house, especially the house. Ben is mad about the garden, but it's the house I want; after this hole it would have made up for everything, everything would have come right between Ben and me. Then you come along to upset it—you're rich and rich people can get things done. I couldn't believe it at first, but Mrs. Barrett told us up at the shop. You mean it, you're going to do it, I know you are!"

Dilys heard herself saying, "Nothing is settled, perhaps something can be arranged." Ben's wife was past reason or hearing. She beat her hands on the table and cried, "Get out of here! Go to hell! Do you hear what I say? Go away!"

It was the only thing to do. Dilys let herself out and walked unsteadily to the entrance and her car. She was deeply disturbed.

She was also very late for lunch.

That afternoon, for Dilys, the garden might have
been in another world. It was withdrawn into a
dreaming stillness and peace. Its colours glowed soft-
ly in the misty air and the sinking sun sent diffused
gold rays slanting through the trees and across the
lawns. Grace had loved autumn and today her garden
had a melancholy beauty, not so much sad, Dilys felt,
as resigned. She did not know how long she spent
wandering there, but by the time she reached the side
garden on the way back to her car, much of the re-
sentments and unhappiness of the last days had fallen
away from her.

Once Mavis had recovered from her annoyance at
Dilys's lateness, she had been kind and sympathetic.
The luncheon was excellent, and it had been a relief
to talk to Mavis; for the first time Dilys had felt that
someone approved of her and what she had done. "Of
course that ridiculous will must be set aside," Mavis
had said. "I hate to disagree with Hugh, but it's not
right. What can have possessed your poor mother?" It

had been obvious that Mavis knew nothing of the letters.

Over coffee they had talked of other things, chiefly of Dilys's children and their doings. Anne, back from France, had found herself a job in London and was no longer living at home but sharing a flat with a friend. "She comes back sometimes at weekends," Dilys said. "I miss her though." Suddenly it occurred to her that it was good of Mavis, who had no children, to listen as she always did with such apparent interest.

Dilys had meant to go back to the King's Arms for a rest before tea. She was tired, something unusual for her; the interview with Ben's wife had upset her. Instead, she had driven round the Green and taken the road that led to the house. Perhaps Mavis's practical common sense had not been reassuring enough, or perhaps Dilys had sensed Mavis's innate dislike and jealousy of Grace. She only knew that she had been seized with an overwhelming longing. As a child, she had always gone to Grace when she was troubled and unhappy. Her stepmother was sometimes brusque and unsympathetic, yet just to be near her was a comfort. If Grace's shade were anywhere, it would be in her garden.

As Dilys walked slowly down the path, she seemed to see Grace vividly, kneeling in her old blue clothes beside the herbaceous border, absorbed and content, needing no one, as she had seen her that May day. It was a day Dilys remembered because Grace had rung her up that evening to tell her that she had found a gardener. Nothing had been the same again.

In Her Garden

Dilys looked up at the walls of the house that repeated the faint pink flush in the western sky. Did she have any deep feeling for Setons now that her life was elsewhere? She had urged Grace to sell it, but that had been for Grace's sake, she had always thought. Now she asked herself if that were true. Was it because she had wanted Grace near her, more dependent on her? Had she always been a little jealous of the garden? Desmond had called her a jealous woman. He had accused her of being jealous of Ben.

Someone was walking down the path behind her, gaining on her at every step. Dilys swung round. All that afternoon she had avoided the kitchen garden where, if he had not gone home, Ben was most likely to be working. The last thing she wanted was an encounter with him. Now here he was.

He did not retreat at the sight of her as he had always done when, on her visits to Grace, she had come across him in the garden. He walked towards her, his head held high, and seemed to her larger, more formidable, than when she had seen him that day in the morning-room. He was wearing dark trousers and a high-necked pullover, and was carrying a jacket. "His good clothes," his wife had said.

As she watched him, Dilys made an effort to see in him something of what Grace must have seen. That he was good-looking, in his fair, stolid way, she had to admit, but to her eyes he was as he had always been, utterly commonplace, loutish, even a little stupid. Then why did she dislike him as she did? What was there about this man that aroused such emotions of love and hate?

He stopped in front of her and said, "What are you doing here?"

It was not said insolently, but calmly, as if he had a right to know. The enmity between them flared up at once, and Dilys's anger against Grace returned. She retorted, "I have as much right to be here as you have."

"Have you? I work here."

Dilys smiled. She said, "So I hear. Why not? You're still the gardener."

She saw him redden, and for a moment she was afraid, but she stood her ground. Dilys was a tall woman and they were much of a height as they faced each other. She had forgotten that his eyes were so intensely blue. At last she said, "I thought you would have gone home by now to see how your little boy was."

To her surprise he. looked away and muttered, "Couldn't face the wife, not after I heard what you had gone and done. The lawyer told me."

"Surely your wife knew already?"

"Not that it was definite."

Dilys, remembering that distraught weeping, was almost sorry for him. She said, "Your wife told me that you had gone to see your lawyer."

He stared at her and said, "What do you mean, she told you? She's been at home all day with Peter."

"I went to see her."

In Her Garden

Ben took a step towards her and said angrily, "You did what? You've got a bloody nerve."

"I thought it only right to talk to her, to find out . . ."

"I bet you found out all right!"

Dilys ignored this. She asked, "What did your lawyer say to you?"

"He told me that Mr. Ransom had got in touch with him and that you had decided to contest the will. He asked me what I wanted to do. I said that I would fight it."

"Was that wise?"

"Wise or not, that's what I'm going to do. I've Peter to think of. I'll fight you all the way, Mrs. Fenton. There'll be no compromise."

"Compromise?"

"That's what Doctor suggested. He came to see me here late this morning, wanting to know like you what Mr. Schofield had said. A good friend he's been to me, has Dr. Grainger. I couldn't go along with him though. 'Settle it out of court,' he said. 'Save a lot of unpleasantness.' He seemed to think that you'd see reason."

"Did he indeed!" Dilys cried. "I can't imagine why. What did he suggest? That I should keep the house and let you have the money?"

"Something like that. I didn't really listen."

Dilys looked up at the house again. She said, "This was my father's house. I was born here. I can't bear to think of a stranger . . ."

In Her Garden

"Then why were you always on at Mrs. Maitland to sell it? She told me."

"That was for her sake . . ." and Dilys said furiously, "So she talked about me to you? How could she?"

Ben interrupted her again; he said, "Listen, Mrs. Fenton. Would you and your children live here? Would you keep up the garden?"

When Dilys did not answer, he said, "I see. It's just that you can't stand the idea of me living here. Well, if that's it, you can bet your life that's that."

He made as if to walk past her, and Dilys stopped him. "You won't win, you know," she said.

"Of course I'll win. Mrs. Maitland left it all to me, and she knew what she was doing."

"She was out of her mind, unbalanced. You saw to that, working on a foolish, lonely old woman."

He lifted his hand and she thought that he was going to hit her. She could see the effort he made to control himself as he said, "You ought to be ashamed of yourself, talking of your mother like that."

"She was not my mother."

Ben looked her in the face. She saw contempt in his eyes. He said, "No. You couldn't have come from someone like her, not you." He put her aside, not roughly but firmly, and walked away.

Too angry for caution, she called after him, "You've gone too far. I know now what to do. Just you wait and see."

He took no notice and she watched him pass

through the archway at the end of the path and out of sight.

When he had gone, she found that she was trembling—was it with anger or fear? Had she really believed that this man had caused Grace's death? She found it easy to believe now.

The silent garden was surrounded by its empty fields. There was not another building between the house and the village over a mile away. She had not seen Ben's van when she arrived, but he usually left it in the yard; she realized now that she had not heard it drive away. The sun had set and twilight had fallen over the garden while she and Ben confronted each other. She could not wait here much longer. Soon it would be dark.

Dilys forced herself to walk on down the path. Passing through the archway was a bad moment; he could be waiting for her on the other side. There was no one in the drive and her car was only a few steps away.

There was still no sign of the van when she drove down the drive, nor was it waiting for her at the gates, as she had half expected. Once out on the road and driving towards the village, she relaxed. It was then that she noticed the headlights in her mirror. They came nearer and nearer, dazzling her. There was no reason why another car should not be on the road with her, even though this road was not much used. Dilys slowed down. There was plenty of room for a car to pass, but nothing passed her. The lights shone steadily behind. In a panic she pressed her foot on the accelerator and shot down the road and into the village. As she rounded the Green, far too fast, she saw that the lights were no longer there.

Dilys parked the car opposite the King's Arms and waited to make sure that no one was following her. Her bag was on the seat beside her and she put her hand out to feel it; of course the letters were still there. The lit windows of the inn shone across the road. She was very tired and, for a moment, was tempted to put off until tomorrow what she had made up her mind to do and, having had a hot bath, to go down to the friendly little bar for a couple of drinks before dinner. By tomorrow her resolution might have weakened. She knew that she must do what she had to do while her anger was still red-hot. She put the car into gear and drove off, taking the road to the town and the police station.

CHAPTER

15

On Friday morning Mrs. Barrett chugged up the
drive on her moped a little before twelve. The mists
and hazy sunshine of the last days had gone and a
strong wind sent the trees above her tossing and com-
plaining under flying clouds. Ben's van was in the
yard but, as usual, there was no sign of him. She let
herself in at the back-door, took off her coat, and unlocked the front. She moved the pile of jumble further out into the hall and went back to the kitchen.
Hope they won't be late, she thought as she made
herself a cup of tea. The house was gloomy on that
grey day and the wind, rattling the windows and
beating on the old walls, filled it with odd noises.
Mrs. Barrett did not hear Dilys open the front door
and cross the hall to the drawing-room.

Dilys had left her car down by the gates and had
walked up the drive in a whirl of dead leaves. She did
not want to see Mrs. Barrett, who, with the rest of
the village, would have heard the latest news about
the will by now. What Dilys had come to the house

to do would take only a few minutes but, having handed over her key to Mr. Ransom, she could not get in unless Mrs. Barrett was there.

Desmond had rung her up after dinner last night to tell her that Anne would be home for the week-end. He had taken it for granted that Dilys would come back as soon as she could. As he had sounded his usual calm, affectionate self and there had been no mention of any quarrel, she had told him that she would leave soon after her appointment with Mr. Ransom. Dilys had gone to bed much happier.

It was only when she woke in the night that she thought of the letters and realized that she would have to tell Desmond what she had done with them. She had not slept again.

After an early breakfast she went straight to the police station. The evening before she had seen only an inspector; this morning the Superintendent was there. It had been no use to ask him to give the letters back to her. He had already read them and thought that at least one of them could be important. He told her very little, yet she had the impression that the police had never been satisfied with the verdict, that they were biding their time and keeping an eye not only on Ben but on everyone else concerned.

When she saw Mr. Ransom, he had been cold and businesslike and quite unsympathetic. Her reasons for taking the letters to the police obviously seemed to him far-fetched. He could not understand why, if she had felt impelled to show them to anyone, she had not brought them to him. He had told her that now that the will was to be contested, nothing further must be taken from the house and had asked for her key. It was then that Dilys had remembered the china dog on the shelf in the caravan. She had forgotten all about it, but suddenly she knew that, Mr. Ransom or not, it was important that she did not go home until she had found out if its counterpart was still in the cabinet in the drawing-room.

It was not yet twelve but, thought Dilys, Mrs. Barrett must already be in the house because the front door was unlocked. Dilys walked as quietly as she could across the hall. The big drawing-room was shadowy and cold on that grey day, and she switched on the light. In the gold-framed mirror above the fireplace something moved, startling her until she saw that it was only the reflection of herself. The china cabinet stood between the two long windows and she went straight to it.

Ever since she could remember, the Staffordshire dog had always sat at the back of the middle shelf. She had been allowed to play with it in the drawing-room but never to take it up to the nursery as she had longed to do. She had not given it a thought for many years, but now she could hear her father saying, "Be careful with it, Dilys. That's quite a valuable little dog."

Having made sure that it was nowhere in the cabinet, Dilys made a quick search of the rest of the room and then stood, frowning and undecided, looking out at the terrace. Peter's mother had said that Ben had bought it in the market. It was possible that Grace had given it to Peter to play with, even had let him take it home.

Dilys turned back to the door. She could have sworn that she had shut it carefully behind her. Now it was wide open. As she reached it and looked out at the empty hall, she knew that someone was in the room above her, in Grace's bedroom. The ceiling shook under running footsteps and there was a thump, as if a chair had been knocked over. Whoever it was was in a hurry, careless of noise. She did not think that it was Mrs. Barrett.

Not caring now if Mrs. Barrett heard her or not, Dilys went quickly across the hall and up the stairs.

The landing and corridor were empty and, as she opened the bedroom door, Dilys thought, I've cornered him now. There was no one in the room, nothing to show that anyone had been there, except for an overturned chair and the Staffordshire dog, sitting on the dressing-table facing her.

Dilys's hand shook as she picked it up. Once again she was being mocked, jeered at. This was without doubt the dog from the china cabinet; she saw the chip on its base that she had made when she dropped it all those years ago. Grace had said, "No, I shouldn't tell your father, if I were you—it's such a tiny chip. Let it be a secret between you and me, and stop that silly crying, you little goose."

Dilys was angry with herself for wasting time. If she had been quicker, she might have caught Ben as he escaped through the dressing-room and bathroom. Although she was sure she was too late, she flung the connecting doors open and ran through them and out into the corridor. There was no one to be seen. He must by now be hurrying down the backstairs and out into the yard.

As she hesitated on the landing, looking down into the hall, the front door bell rang. She put her hand on the stair-rail, wondering if she ought to go down and answer it, but Mrs. Barrett forestalled her. A car from the village had come to collect the jumble.

Dilys waited where she was and watched Mrs. Barrett and two women she did not recognize carry the boxes and piles of clothes out to a waiting car. Their voices came up to her, but she did not listen; she was wondering impatiently how soon she could make her own escape. If she used the backstairs, Ben might still be lurking in the yard.

The attack, when it came, took her completely by surprise. There was no sound behind her, no movement that she could later remember, only the violent blow between the shoulder-blades that sent her forward and down. At the turn of the stairs, she tried to catch hold of the banister, but her weight carried her on. She was conscious of an agonizing pain in her wrist, and nothing more.

Dilys was heavy and the shock of her fall resounded through the house. Mrs. Barrett screamed.

When Dilys opened her eyes, she was lying at the bottom of the stairs. Someone had put a cushion under her head and she was being covered with a blanket. Mrs. Barrett's face looked down at her, coming nearer and then retreating into whirling mists again. Other people were there. She heard voices. Someone was saying, "Mrs. Fenton, Mrs. Fenton," over and over again; she made no attempt to answer. Then Hugh was there, kneeling beside her, and behind him she saw Ben. The hall steadied round her as she looked up at them.

Hugh's hands were going over her, gently and expertly. She cried out once with pain and he said, "Don't move." After a few moments he said, in his usual bantering way, "Well, Dilys, what do you think you're doing, falling about like that, giving us all such a fright?"

"I didn't fall," she said as loudly as she could. "I was pushed."

At once babel broke out round her. Someone said, "It's the shock," and Mrs. Barrett cried, "I didn't even know Mrs. Fenton was in the house until she came tumbling down those stairs. There was no one else there, no one on the landing. That's true, I'll swear."

Dilys tried to sit up, but Hugh restrained her. He said, "You must lie still until the ambulance comes. Your wrist is fractured and you've hurt your back. I don't think it's serious, probably only a sprain. You've had a nasty fall, but you've been lucky."

"Grace wasn't lucky," Dilys said. "She broke her neck."

In Her Garden

Hugh went on as if she hadn't spoken, "I'll go with you to hospital; that wrist must be X-rayed, for one thing. If they want to keep you in for a bit, Mavis will bring your things from the pub; if not, you must come to us and she will look after you. Leave it all to me and don't worry. I'll ring Desmond."

She pushed his hand away and cried, "Send for the police. It was Ben. He tried to kill me."

There was a stunned silence, then Mrs. Barrett said, "Poor soul, she doesn't know what she's saying. Take no notice."

Hugh looked up at Ben, who met his gaze gravely, and slowly shook his head. He had come running when he heard Mrs. Barrett shouting for him and, kicking off his boots in the scullery, had hurried into the hall and now stood there in his socks. It was Ben who had telephoned for Hugh and then had insisted that Dilys must not be moved until he came. Now he said, "That's a wicked thing to say, Mrs. Fenton, and you know as well as I do it isn't true. I haven't been in the house for weeks."

Dilys said, "He was in Grace's bedroom, I heard him there, and then he must have hidden behind the curtains on the landing. Mrs. Barrett knows that he has often been in the house."

"I don't know any such thing," Mrs. Barrett said. "Someone got in days ago, through the pantry window. It could have been anyone."

"It was Ben," Dilys repeated. "On Monday, Wednesday, and today he was in the house again. I heard him at the drawing-room door but when I looked into the hall it was empty; he ran upstairs when he saw me. Ben, why did you put the dog on the dressing-table?"

He stared at her in bewilderment and Mrs. Barrett said, "She's out of her mind—what dog?"

"It's still there. Go upstairs and fetch it, Mrs. Barrett. Then perhaps you will all believe me."

Mrs. Barrett looked at Hugh, who signed to her to do as Dilys asked. No one spoke, or moved, until Mrs. Barrett came back. She was carrying the little china dog, held well away from her as if it might explode at any moment.

Ben took a step towards her. He said, "That's Peter's dog," and stopped. His usually ruddy face paled as they all looked at him.

"You meant to put it back in the cabinet where it belongs, didn't you?" Dilys said. "Your wife told you that I had seen it in the caravan; she said you had bought it in the market. You're a thief as well as everything else—you took that dog and you took the painting. Look at him, all of you, look at his face! Surely you believe me? You must, you must!"

Hugh said, "Gently, Dilys. Hysterics won't help you or anyone else."

She clutched his arm and said, "Help me up. If no one else will telephone for the police, I will."

Ben moved at last. A little colour had come back into his face. "I'll ring them myself," he said.

"Tell them there's been an accident," Hugh said. "Don't say anything else."

Ben nodded and, as he went towards the morning-room, moving in a dazed way, Dilys cried, "Don't let him out of your sight, Hugh. He'll get away."

Ben turned and looked back. He gave them a travesty of a smile. "Not to worry, Doctor," he said. "I haven't taken leave of my senses even if she has."

The ambulance and the police car arrived at the same time. Hugh told the officers why they had been summoned while the ambulance men waited with their stretcher. "I know Ben Halden well," Hugh added. "Mrs. Fenton's accusation is absurd. She's badly shocked and can't realize what she's saying. I must insist that, as my patient, she is moved at once. Surely you could get a full statement from her in hospital? She's in no condition to make one now."

Dilys, looking up at the two policemen, asked loudly, "Why don't you arrest Ben at once? He tried to kill me—kill me, do you hear?" As they signed to the ambulance men to bring the stretcher, she said, "No, no! Fetch the Superintendent. I must see the Superintendent—he knows all about it. I saw him at the station yesterday."

"Dilys, you didn't, you wouldn't?" Hugh cried, and checked himself. She turned her head towards him and said, "I did."

Hugh had been so certain that, when it came to it, Dilys would never bring herself to show Grace's letters to the police that now he could not bear to look at her as she was lifted onto the stretcher and carried away.

Having given his name and address and a brief

statement, he was allowed to follow her in his car. At the door he looked back. The three women had drawn together as the officer approached them with his notebook. Ben stood a little apart, a lonely figure. He had so far said nothing in his defence and waited impassively. Hugh felt that he was deserting him, and he called, "Don't look like that, Ben. I don't think you have much to worry about, but I'd get in touch with Mr. Schofield if I were you."

As he followed the ambulance down the drive he wondered what the police would do. Mrs. Barrett and the two women would probably be allowed to go home directly they had given their statements. What a wagging of tongues there would then be! What they had to tell would spread like wildfire through the village. Hugh meant to ring Mavis up from the hospital, but by that time she would probably have heard all about it. As for Ben, would he eventually be allowed to go home too, or would he be taken to the police station for further questioning? In which case, who would tell that wretched little wife of his where he was?

The wind had dropped and it was raining heavily. Hugh groaned. He foresaw a busy, probably luncheonless, and most distressing afternoon.

CHAPTER

16

The wildest rumours circulated through the village all that weekend, as Hugh had foreseen: Ben Halden had assaulted Mrs. Fenton and thrown her down the stairs at Setons; she was now in hospital with a broken back. Mrs. Fenton had discovered Ben taking valuables from the drawing-room and, with Mrs. Barrett's assistance, had held him until the police arrived. Setons had been ransacked by vandals. Oddly enough, nothing had been said or even hinted as to Grace's death, perhaps because that was in the past and the present was exciting enough.

By Monday morning, sober facts began to emerge. How disappointing that was! It was known that Mrs. Fenton had been discharged from hospital on Saturday and was staying at the doctor's; her husband and daughter had been down from London to see her. Ben had been seen driving through the village on his way to work, and his wife was back in the shop, where Mrs. Roper kept her in the background, unpacking stores, well away from curious eyes. Mrs. Barrett's husband had declared that he would not allow her to go back to that Setons again, but soon after nine that same Monday she was chugging up the drive as usual.

When, later that morning, Mrs. Barrett tried to ring up Hugh, he was out, so Mavis was the first to learn that the police had been to the house and had taken Ben to the police station. Mrs. Barrett then rang up Mrs. Roper at the shop and soon this fresh news spread through the village.

Hugh, having arranged for Dr. Sands to take morning surgery, was already on his way to Setons. All that week-end he had been worried about Ben. On Friday, after leaving the hospital, he had gone to find him as he wanted to know how Ben had fared with the two policemen and what had happened after the ambulance left. It was growing late, as Hugh had waited to know the results of the X-rays and, as the Site was on his way, he had tried the caravan first. Ben's wife, who had been giving Peter his tea, had come to the door; Hugh had thought that she looked ill and was thinner than ever. He had told her nothing about Dilys's accident, and when she said that her husband had not come home, that he was usually later than this, Hugh had decided to look for Ben in the garden. If Ben was not there, Hugh had thought, he would come home himself and ring up the police station. He had met the white van at the bottom of the drive. It was beginning to grow dark and it had been difficult to see Ben's face, but his manner had been strange, surly, and uncommunicative; he had barely answered when questioned. "Very well, Ben," Hugh had said at last. "Go home now and try to have a good night's sleep."

Now, as Hugh drove into the yard and parked beside the van, Mrs. Barrett ran out of the back-door. She was agitated and incoherent, and it took a few minutes before he could make out what she was trying to tell him.

"Helping them with their enquiries, that's what Ben is doing, or so they said when I asked the officer if they were arresting him. I told the sergeant, or whoever he was, that they were making a silly mistake. Mrs. Fenton tripped and fell, that's what she did, and why should they think different? They wouldn't listen to me. You go and tell them, Doctor."

Hugh managed to quieten her, and persuaded her to go back to the kitchen while he telephoned Mr. Schofield.

Mr. Schofield sounded perturbed as he said that yes, Ben Halden had had the sense to ask for him and he was about to leave for the police station. "Surely they won't hold Ben for long?" Hugh asked. "It's an absurd accusation." "That depends," Mr. Schofield answered. "Some evidence that we know nothing about may have come to light. Ring me up at the police station, say, in about an hour, and I'll let you know what transpires."

Hugh felt the need to calm himself if he was to think clearly, as he must do if he wanted to help

In Her Garden

Ben. To avoid Mrs. Barrett, he let himself out of the drawing-room windows and walked up and down the terrace, his hands in the pockets of the tweed overcoat Mavis had made him wear. The wind and rain of yesterday had gone, but it was a grey, cold, and depressing day. He asked himself why he was so sure that Ben was innocent, not only of this last accusation, but in all his dealings with Grace. Was it possible that he had been mistaken all along and that Ben was the calculating schemer that Dilys thought him? Could Grace have loved such a man? Women were notoriously blind where the men they loved were concerned, but he had always trusted Grace's judgement.

Hugh found that he was thinking of Grace with longing, as Dilys had done. Her imprint was everywhere in her garden, and he wondered if it would ever fade for those who had known her well. He thought of her letters to Ben, now with the police. I should have managed somehow to stop Dilys, he thought, to prevent her—he would never forgive himself, or Dilys, who was now a guest in his house. She was Mavis's friend, and he liked Desmond.

He frowned as he considered Dilys. She had been so positive that her fall was no accident that he himself was almost convinced, as perhaps the police were. If what Dilys said were true, then someone had done it, had deliberately tried to kill her. I can't believe it of Ben, Hugh thought. Then who?

Hugh came to an abrupt halt. He lifted his head and looked across the lawn. Of course!

In Her Garden

Hugh went back through the drawing-room into the hall. He knew now what he must do; first, though, he would have to think how to set about it. Deep in thought, he did not at once hear Mrs. Barrett calling, "Doctor! Doctor!"

She was standing in the kitchen doorway and she cried again, "Doctor, come quickly! See what I've found."

She had laid the little canvas down on the kitchen table. Someone had slashed it from side to side, slashed it again and again. As Hugh picked it up, Mrs. Barrett said, "It's one of Mrs. Maitland's paintings, isn't it? What a wicked shame! Who could have done a thing like that?"

Hugh said slowly, "I think I know." He looked down at what once had been a painting. "Yes, I was right. Where did you find it, Mrs. Barrett?"

"In the broom cupboard in the scullery, and the knife what did it was there too, chucked in as if whoever it was was in a hurry. One of our own kitchen knives."

Mrs. Barrett sat down on the nearest chair. "What a morning," she said. "First Ben and the police, and now this. I think I'll go home. I don't like this house anymore. What Bert will say when he hears about it, I can guess."

"You've had a shock, and I'm sorry," Hugh said. "I should certainly go home now and have a rest. I'll wait while you lock up and see you safely off the premises."

"What about that?" Mrs. Barrett asked, pointing at the canvas.

"Don't you worry. I'll take it with me, not that there's anything I can do, it's past saving."

"Will you let Mrs. Fenton know? And the police?"

"Of course. Now please hurry, Mrs. Barrett. I have a lot to do this morning."

Hugh drove towards the village, trying to decide on his next move. He parked his car outside the King's Arms, went into the bar, and sat with a drink in a corner, looking so unapproachable that no one dared to speak to him. After looking at his watch, he put his empty glass down on the counter and, with a nod to the barman, went to telephone the police station. Curious eyes followed him. "What's up with Doctor?" someone asked.

It was a few minutes before he was allowed to speak to Mr. Schofield. It seemed that new evidence had indeed come to light, but it concerned the Wednesday when Grace had died. As Ben's bad luck would have it, a passing police car, whose driver had given it no thought at the time, had seen the white van turning into Setons' drive. Ben could only say that on his way home from the doctor's he had remembered that he had left all the windows in the greenhouses open. As late September nights could be chilly, he had dropped by to close them and, in the shock of Mrs. Maitland's death, had forgotten all about it. "Rather thin, I fear," Mr. Schofield said. "I can see that the police don't believe a word of it."

Hugh looked grim as he got into his car. This was a setback. Could he be wrong? It was Wednesday, Mr. Schofield had said. Among Grace's letters to Ben, there had been one about a Wednesday afternoon. He remembered now.

He went first to the shop, which was even more crowded than usual. Mrs. Roper came to meet him. "If you're looking for Sandra, she's not here," he was told. "I took her home after Mrs. Barrett telephoned. Terrible state she was in. She hasn't been herself for some time, not since she heard about the upset over the will, but today she quite broke down. Wouldn't let me stay with her though, said she wanted to be alone. I rang up when I got back to ask you to have a look at her. Mrs. Grainger took the message."

Mrs. Roper paused for breath and Hugh said, "I'll go at once. Thank you, Mrs. Roper," but Mrs. Roper hadn't finished. "What can the police be thinking of?" she asked him. "Why should they believe Mrs. Fenton, nothing but trouble she is. Ben's not much good, but he wouldn't go and do a daft thing like that, why should he?" There were murmurs from the crowd, and Hugh made his escape.

Unlike Grace and Dilys, he did not leave his car at the entrance to the Site, but drove up to the steps of the Haldens' caravan. When he knocked, there was no reply. He knocked again and a voice called, "Go away." He thought that the door was bound to be locked, yet when he turned the handle, it swung open.

Ben's wife was not lying face down on her bed as he had imagined she would be. She was sitting at the table, her hands clenched before her on the cloth. The curtains had been drawn across the windows and her face was a white blur in the gloom. The first thing Hugh did was to pull the curtains back. Then he sat down opposite her.

Now that he could see her clearly he was shocked; it was such a haggard and desperate young face. The circles under the huge eyes were as dark as bruises and the dead white skin looked dry and paper-thin over the high cheek-bones. She stared back at him with a sort of dumb defiance that made him think of some wretched little animal at bay in its hole.

He put his large, warm hand over her cold ones and said, "Your aunt asked me to come and see you. She is worried about you."

Sandra pulled her hands away and said in her hoarse childlike voice, "I'm all right. I don't need no doctor. Why can't she mind her own business?"

Hugh looked round the untidy room and said, "Where's Peter?"

"At school, of course. Where else would he be?"

"When will he be back?"

"Round half-past three."

"Good. That gives us plenty of time."

In Her Garden

"Time for what?"

"To get to the bottom of this most unhappy affair."

"I don't know what you mean."

She had drawn back, and was there a flicker of alarm in those opaque eyes? She cried, "Ben has been arrested. He's at the police station. Can't you have the decency to leave me alone?"

"Ben hasn't been arrested, he's being questioned. Helping the police with their enquiries."

"What's the difference?"

"Quite a bit. I wonder why you didn't ask your aunt to drive you to the police station. Most wives would have rushed off to their husbands at once."

She hung her head and did not answer. Hugh said, "You didn't want to see him, did you? I wonder why."

"I wasn't up to it. I was all in."

"You couldn't face him, I suppose." Hugh's voice was still gentle even when he said, "Sit up, Sandra. Look at me and pay attention. What did Ben tell you when he came home on Friday?"

She put her hair back from her face and sat up obediently. "He told me nothing," she said. "He wouldn't even speak to me. I didn't know about Mrs. Fenton until I went to the shop Saturday morning."

"Where were you on Friday then? The whole village knew it that very afternoon and those old gossips at the shop would have been full of it."

"I wasn't there. I was here. My auntie sent me

home in the morning because I wasn't feeling well."

"How did you get here?"

"I had my bike, hadn't I? Days I don't get a lift I bicycle to the shop. Ben could have easily fitted in with me and dropped me off on his way to work. He needn't have gone off all that early if he hadn't wanted to, but he did want to, and it didn't matter about me. Selfish, bloody selfish, that's what he is, always has been. And now look what he's gone and done. Pushing people downstairs—not that I blame him. Wicked she is, trying to take the house away from us."

All this was said in an aggrieved whine and Hugh's heart hardened. He said, "Ben didn't do it. We both know that, don't we? And we both know that you were in the house that morning."

The girl jumped up. She backed away from him and cried, "Me? What would I be doing there, I ask you?"

"Putting that china dog back. Mrs. Fenton had seen it and recognized it. You were afraid."

The girl stared at him and said nothing. Hugh went on, "I wonder why you didn't put it back on Thursday afternoon. Was it because it would have been difficult to get into the house, or was it because you thought Ben might come home early and find that you had left Peter here alone? He wouldn't have liked that, would he? Friday was far safer. All you had to do was pretend to be ill and then bicycle from the shop to the house."

"I didn't, I didn't. I came straight back here."

In Her Garden

Hugh took no notice. He said, "You had been in the house several times before. Once you got in through the pantry window. At other times Mrs. Barrett was there and you could sneak in through the back-door."

"Well, what if I did? I was just looking."

"You usually went on a Wednesday, didn't you, when the shop was shut and you knew Ben was working for me?"

"Yes, but I went other days too. I would take the short cut through the orchard, find out where Ben was, and then, if I couldn't get in, go round the outside of the house looking in at the windows. It was going to be our house soon, wasn't it, and I wanted to see what it was like. What was the harm in that?"

"None, so far, but what about that painting, Sandra?"

"What painting? What do you mean?"

"You know very well. You took it, didn't you?"

After a pause, Sandra said, "What if I did? That old bitch went and painted my Ben—she had no bloody business to go and do that. I was going round the front of the house—a Monday it was. Ben was cutting a hedge at the bottom of the garden so I knew I was safe. I saw Mrs. Fenton sitting at a writing-table in the window. She gave me a start I can tell you, but her back was turned and she didn't see me watching her. Every so often, she'd get up and go to the other side of the room, and once she picked up something from the settee and stood there staring at it. I couldn't see what it was and I wanted to know."

168

"So you went into the house. How did you get in?"

"Through the front door of course; she had left it unlocked."

"And then what did you do?"

"I hid on the landing until I saw her come out and go into the kitchen. Then I nipped down and went straight to the settee. There was the painting, with Ben on a mower—my Ben. I picked it up and ran upstairs—a near thing it was because Mrs. Fenton came back in a few minutes."

"You hid until Mrs. Fenton had gone, and then you took the painting into the kitchen. Why?"

"I wanted a knife."

Sandra looked defiantly at Hugh. "I enjoyed it," she said. "I liked using that knife. I cut and cut, and then threw what was left of that bloody painting into the broom cupboard and got out fast. I was afraid Ben might be home before me."

There was a pause. Hugh controlled himself. To say what he thought would be useless and might drive her into obstinate silence. He said, as calmly as he could, "What about that other time, last Wednesday afternoon, when you tried to frighten Mrs. Fenton? She told my wife all about it. You walked about upstairs and you made a noise on the piano. That was naughty of you."

Sandra smiled, a grim little smile. "Serve her right. She shouldn't have come back after Mrs. Barrett had gone. Gave me quite a turn, she did. Nearly caught me on the stairs."

As she sat down again and faced him, Hugh saw that it had been a mistake to be gentle with her. She was tougher than she looked.

He leant forward and said sternly, "And now we come to Friday. How did you know that Mrs. Barrett would be there that morning and you would be able to get in?"

"I heard them talking Wednesday. Something about the jumble and her being there round twelve."

"You found the front door open. If you had seen Mrs. Fenton's car left by the gates, you would have been more cautious, so you must have left your bicycle in the lane and taken the short cut through the orchard. It must have been a shock to find her in the drawing-room. You sneaked upstairs and left the china dog on the dressing-table. You heard Mrs. Fenton coming after you and you hid."

"I didn't. I wasn't up there. It must have been someone else."

She looked round wildly, as if the caravan were a trap closing on her and cried, "Ben! It must have been Ben."

Now she was really afraid, near to breaking point. Her hands were clenched, her small nostrils dilated. He said, "You shouldn't have said that, Sandra."

The huge black eyes were searching his face imploringly. He felt not even a shred of pity, only contempt, and she knew it. Putting her hands over her face she began to cry.

Hugh sat still and let her cry. Tears were streaming down her face, taking with them, he hoped, the last of her resistance. When they lessened, he handed her his clean white handkerchief and, as she clutched it and wiped her eyes, said, "Come on, Sandra, tell me, or do you want me to tell you? Very well, I will. Mrs. Fenton was standing at the top of the stairs. Where were you? On the window-seat behind the curtain? You must have been."

She nodded, and at last said, "There she was, leaning on the stair-rail, looking down. It was easy. One good quick push and down she went, making enough noise to wake the dead. I heard Mrs. Barrett in the hall but I didn't wait. I ran down the corridor to the backstairs and across the garden. I knew Ben was somewhere about and I prayed he wouldn't see me. I thought to myself, That's an end to our troubles. I thought she was dead, you see."

Hugh said nothing. He looked at her steadily and she began to fidget. The silence in the room was too much for her and she cried. "What more do you want? I've told you . . ."

"You haven't told me everything. What about that time when Mrs. Maitland died? You were there in the garden, hanging about the place, spying on her, as you'd done before. What happened that day?"

The effect of this was startling. He had not thought it possible that she could become even paler. Her pinched small face was so livid that he was afraid she was going to faint.

As he stretched out a hand to her, she shrank away

from him and said, "Don't—I didn't mean to do it. She shouldn't of called me a child—I'm not a child, I'm Ben's wife."

Hugh waited, afraid to move, holding his breath. Her eyes, fixed on his face, were imploring again; he made no attempt to help her. She gave a strangled sob and said, "I'd been following her through the orchard. She didn't see me but she knew someone was there, she called out once, and I thought I'd got her rattled. It was in that place with the roses that I caught up with her. She was at the bottom of the steps when she turned and saw me behind her. She said, 'What are you doing here?'

" 'I've got something to say to you,' I told her. 'If you know what's good for you, leave my husband alone.' She looked at me then as if she was sorry for me. 'My poor child,' she said, superior and condescending—superior, her! 'You still love him, don't you? You're jealous, jealous of an old woman like me. I should feel flattered.' I lost my temper then. I called her names. I said, 'You bloody, disgusting old bitch, I know what you're up to—at your age,' and then . . ." Sandra caught her breath.

"And then?" Hugh said gently.

"Then she turned her back on me and went up the steps. I ran and got in front of her. I was that angry I hardly knew what I was doing."

Hugh closed his eyes as if to shut out that scene, which was becoming unbearably vivid; he could almost smell the roses.

In Her Garden

"You hit her? Pushed her?"

"Must have done, mustn't I? There she was at the bottom of the steps, dead."

After a moment Hugh said, "How did you know? Did you make sure before you went away and left her there?"

"She was dead all right. Her eyes looked up at me. I saw the life go out of them. It was horrible, horrible. I haven't been able to sleep proper ever since."

Hugh sighed. He felt tired and suddenly old. There was much that he could have said, but what was the use? He had what he wanted. It remained to be seen what would happen when he took Sandra to the police station. Would she deny everything she had said to him? He did not think so, but he could not be sure.

She sat with her head drooping, the black hair hiding her face, exhaustion in every line of her. He said, "You feel better, don't you, now that you've got that off your chest? You've been longing to tell someone."

The tears began again, slow, difficult tears this time. He waited a moment and then stood up. "Fetch your coat," he said.

She looked up at him, dazed and bewildered. "My coat? Why? Where are we going?"

"I'm going to drive you to the police station."

"No! I've told you. I don't want to see Ben."

"You needn't see him. I'm sure that can be arranged. All you've got to do is to tell the police what you've told me."

In Her Garden

She shrank away from him and cried, "I won't, I won't. I'll say you made it all up to help Ben. I'll say you made me say it."

Hugh looked down at her from his impressive height. He said, "And who do you think they'll believe, you or me?"

The fight went out of her. She said, "You, of course. It isn't fair."

Her gaze went round the room, as if looking for a way out and finding none. She said, "They'll put me in prison. I'll go to prison, won't I?"

Hugh did not answer. Attempted murder and, would it be, manslaughter? How many years could she get for that? If there was any question of bail he supposed that the Ropers would see to it; ironically, with all that was hanging in the balance for him, Ben had no money.

"Oh well," Sandra said wearily as she got to her feet. "Prison might be better than being here with Ben once he knows."

"Ben has no reason to care about Mrs. Fenton," Hugh said.

"I wasn't thinking of her."

He found a coat in the cupboard of the next room. As he helped her into it, she said, "They'll let Ben go soon, won't they?"

"I expect so."

Would Ben refuse even to see Sandra once he knew how Grace had died? That he would do what was necessary to help her, Hugh was sure. "She's my wife after all," Ben had once said. He was sure, too, that as soon as possible, Ben would take Peter and leave the village, go as far away as he could from all of them.

Hugh looked down at Sandra and asked her, "Would you really have said nothing and let Ben go to prison in your place?"

She gave a little shrug. "Perhaps not. I don't know. What does it matter now?"

As she buttoned her coat, she looked up at him and said, "You'll stay with me, won't you? At the police station, I mean," and put her hand in his.

Hugh was touched, in spite of himself. "If I can. They may not let me."

She sighed and said, "Come on then, let's get it over."

At the door he paused. "What about Peter?" he asked.

"What about him?"

"He'll be back from school soon. The caravan will be locked."

"Peter will be all right. Someone will look after him until Ben gets back."

"Ben may be some time. I'll ring up my wife from the police station and ask her to fetch Peter. She loves children."

There was no response, and Hugh, releasing her hand from his, opened the door.

He had hoped that as it must be time for the midday meal, everyone on the Site would be indoors, and he was annoyed to find that a small crowd had gathered near his car to stare at the caravan. In the foreground was a long-haired girl wheeling a pram and a woman in a flowered overall who held a small ginger-haired boy by the hand. Sandra shrank back against him then as he took her arm, stepped down, and, her head high, walked unsteadily to the car.

Hugh locked the caravan, put the key in his pocket, and, ignoring the avid stares, got into the driving seat. The small boy, an irrepressible child he had often seen in the surgery, darted forward.

"Where are you taking her, Doc?" he asked. "To hospital?"

There were murmurs, perhaps of sympathy, from the onlookers. The police, inquiring for Ben, would have called earlier at the Site, to be followed not long after by Mrs. Roper bringing her niece home. The village grapevine would have worked at its usual speed and probably all these people knew where Ben was. No wonder that there was curiosity and excited speculation.

Nothing to what there will be soon, Hugh thought grimly.

In the car the girl spoke twice. After a long silence she asked, "Will I be in the papers, my picture and all?"

"Very likely."

His answer appeared to satisfy her. She was quiet until they were nearly there. Then she said, "What will Mrs. Fenton do now? About the house and money, I mean? Could this make a difference?"

Hugh said cautiously, "It might. I don't know, of course, but it might." And he added, "I think it will."

176

It was beginning to snow again when Hugh turned his car into the drive. Someone had driven up to the house before him—there were tyre marks in the snow—but he was surprised to find Mrs. Barrett in the yard, trying to coax her moped to start.

"I thought you had given up working here," he said as he got out of his warm car. The January day was the coldest so far that winter and he shivered even in his padded topcoat and fur hat.

"I have, Bert made me," Mrs. Barrett said. "I've kept away for weeks, but today I was passing and I thought I'd drop in for a last look round. Silly really, but here I am."

"And here I am," Hugh said, "doing much the same. We are drawn back, aren't we, in spite of ourselves? This is the last time though. This is good-bye."

"For me, too. We aren't the only ones, Doctor. Ben's here."

In Her Garden

"Ben?" Hugh looked round. "How did he get here?"

"Same old van, he's put it into the garage to keep warm. He can't have got the money yet, or the house for that matter. This probate, or whatever they call it, takes ages, I've heard, not that Ben will ever live here. The house will be up for sale, I suppose. Well, he's somewhere in the garden."

"I'll look for him. Are you all right, Mrs. Barrett?"

"I'm fine now this dratted machine's started. Bye-bye, Doctor." Mr. Barrett, so heavily wrapped up in coats and scarfs that she looked almost square, spluttered off round the house.

Hugh crossed the lawn, the light, frosted snow of last night's fall crunching under his feet. He thought he knew where Ben would be, and he was right.

Ben was in the rose garden. He stood by the big centre bed, looking through the gap in the yew hedge at the snowy orchard beyond. He swung round, startled, as Hugh came down the steps.

Hugh thought that Ben looked much older. He had lost his ruddy glow and was thin and drawn, but his bare head against the dark yew had lost none of its fairness. He was wearing a dark overcoat with the collar turned up.

"Ben! I'm glad to see you," Hugh said. "I'd begun to think I never would again."

"I should have come to you, Doctor," Ben said, "to thank you for all you've done, and for being such a friend to me. I couldn't face the village, that's a fact."

In Her Garden

"I don't want thanking, Ben. I would have liked though to have known where you were and how you are."

"I'm all right. I've got a job, had to. The money isn't mine yet, although Mr. Ransom offered me an advance. I'm working on the roads, it's not much but it's hard and does me good."

"How is Peter?"

"He's fine. I've got rooms in a farmhouse, real country, a good way from here so he goes to another school, but he likes it and the farm people are good to him. One day, when it's all settled, Peter and I will look round for a place of our own, with a bit of land. Maybe I'll run a market garden, or greenhouses, something like that. I would of liked him to grow up here, but that's impossible."

Hugh said, "It must be good to know that now you will be able to do a lot for Peter."

"Yes, give him everything I never had. She—Mrs. Maitland—would be glad of that, wouldn't she? Some good has come out of it all."

It was too cold to stand still any longer, and they began to walk up and down. "Do you come here often, Ben?" Hugh asked. "To the garden, I mean."

"Not often. Now and again at weekends. That firm, Lawns, or whatever they're called, look after it now, Mr. Ransom arranged it. I won't come again, though. It's no use hanging about, I've got to make the break."

Hugh thought, And so have I. Mrs. Barrett too— we all feel it's time.

He said, after a few minutes, "It's damn cold here. I suppose the greenhouses are locked?"

"Yes, I tried them."

"I'll go home then. I suppose it's no use asking you to come with me for a drink? No? Well then, I'll say goodbye. Keep in touch, won't you?"

"I will that, Doctor."

Hugh held out his hand and, as Ben took it, Hugh said, "There's something I must ask before I go. Do you ever see Sandra?"

Ben released Hugh's hand and looked away. He said, "No. I can't bring myself to do that yet. Her aunt goes and so does old Roper, so Mrs. Barrett told me. It seems they have made out it's all my fault and that's a comfort to them!"

"What will happen to Sandra?"

"I suppose, when the time comes, I'll have to go and fetch her."

"Ben! After all that . . ."

"Should have to, shouldn't I? She'll still be my wife. Sandra will be on about Setons even then, I'm sure. But she'll never come here, never. Not here!"

There was nothing more to say and Hugh turned to go. "Coming too, Ben?" he said.

"You go on, Doctor. I'll come in a moment."

As Hugh climbed the steps, he looked back. Ben was standing where he had first seen him, his hands in his pockets, his head bent. Snow was falling steadily now, and Hugh left him there alone, as Ben, for that moment, wished to be.

CHAPTER

18

The blank, curtainless windows of the house reflected the skies of early summer where the swallows swooped about their business as they had always done. The garden drowsed in its sun-warmed peace after the snows and turmoil of a long, hard winter. Nothing much had changed, although the hedges were perhaps shaggier, the lawns less smooth than they once had been, the flower beds beginning to be full of weeds.

The drive wound down to the gates, which were now kept closed. Here, displayed for anyone passing in the road to see, was a board bearing in large white letters the words FOR SALE.

A   NOTE   ABOUT   THE   AUTHOR

Jon Godden was born in Bengal and is the eldest of four sisters,
the second of whom is Rumer Godden. Her parents lived for
many years in India, and she herself lived alternately there and in
England. She began to write in 1938 when she was living in Cal-
cutta, and her novels have received high praise on both sides of
the Atlantic. She now makes her home in Kent. Her novels in-
clude *The House by the Sea, The Peacock, The City and the Wave, The
Seven Islands, Mrs. Panopoulis,* and *A Winter's Tale.*

A NOTE ON THE TYPE

The text of this book was set in a film version of Garamond. The
design is based on letter forms originally created by Claude Garamond (1510–1561). Garamond was a pupil of Geoffroy Tory
and may have patterned his letter forms on Venetican models. To
this day, the typeface that bears his name is one of the most attractive used in book composition, and the intervening years have
caused it to lose little of its freshness or beauty.

Composed by Publishers Phototype, Inc.,
Carlstadt, New Jersey
Printed and bound by American Book-Stratford Press,
Saddle Brook, New Jersey

Designed by Judith Henry